Praise for Drag

———— ✦ ————

"When my daughter was in her bedtime-story years, she LOVED great storytelling but could spot one that had a too-obvious "moral" to the story a mile away. With *Dragon Magic*, Jan Ögren has given us a set of tales and adventure stories for both children and adults that masterfully speak to the beauty and potential of the human spirit, without ever becoming preachy or feeling like lessons. I highly recommend this book for parents of young children and educators – AND I'm putting it on my bedside table to remind me to stay in a state of wonder and mystery as I make my way through each day."

> **Cassandra Vieten**, President/CEO, Institute of Noetic Sciences and author of *Mindful Motherhood: Practical Tools for Staying Sane During Pregnancy and Your Child's First Year*. Co-author of *Living Deeply*

———— ✦ ————

"*Dragon Magic* is a collection of delightful stories appropriate for both children and adults. In today's technical world, it is important and exciting to provide these charming avenues into magic. Magic that is not occurring in some supernatural realm but that is happening right here within and around us in our own wonderful natural world and in the amazing discoveries of our own postmodern sciences. Magic that all of us can see, hear, and feel if we will just pay close attention with all of our senses. I was especially drawn to the "Dragon Magic" story, because it begins with the great mythic beasts of our imagination and leads us into our own backyards, showing us the amazing connectedness and communication that exists when we look with care and wonder at ourselves and our world."

> **Unitarian Universalist Minister Rev. Shirley Ranck**, author of *Cakes for the Queen of Heaven: An Exploration of Women's Power Past, Present, and Future* and *The Grandmother Galaxy: A Journey into Feminist Spirituality*

"Jan Ögren has put together a collection of inspired and inspirational stories. These tales told in the spirit of the oral traditions are teaching stories as well as adventures. They offer us advice and wisdom drawn from a keen observation of nature. They show us ways to face challenges and obstacles with imagination. It is so important to nurture the creative spirit in our young ones so that they may grow healthy and joyful. Jan has accomplished this in her stories. This book is a gift for all ages."

> **Lucy Lewis** is a dancer, artist, anthropologist, and co-coordinator of the International Conference on Shamanism, Healing, and Transformation

———— ✦ ————

"To survive, human beings need food, shelter, clothing, and stories. Why stories? Because stories give meaning to one's life: they bond communities and they facilitate communication. Jan Ögren is a master story-teller, and I have heard her oral presentations of many of the tales in this marvelous book. For those readers who have not been fortunate enough to have heard Jan in person, this book is the next best option. Jan knows how to entertain, but her narratives also have deeper meanings that reflect the very core of human existence. Even though many of these stores take place in an unspecified time and place, they are all relevant for today's world, one in which people need all the instruction they can get if they are to get through these tough times alive."

> **Stanley Krippner, Ph.D.**, Professor of Psychology at Saybrook University in San Francisco. Krippner is a pioneer in the study of consciousness. Co-author, *Healing Tales: The Narrative Arts in Spiritual Traditions* and *Personal Mythology: The Psychology of Your Evolving Self*

"The fables Jan Ögren has fashioned feel so ancient and universal that I found myself referring to one yesterday as if it were common knowledge. I started to talk about Wizard Agatha's spell as if my colleagues would know it in the same way that they know the Tortoise and the Hare, or "crying wolf." I stopped myself with a laugh and explained that they need to read *Dragon Magic* so that they too will know these characters who feel so alive and real to me.

I want these fables to take their place in the world. I want everyone to know these tales so that I can refer to Wizard Agatha's spell, the Blind Bunny, and to the Life-Glows inside all of us and be understood. What I love most, as an avid reader, is to learn through stories. Jan has created a cast of characters that will live in the minds and hearts of future readers for generations to come, as they now live in mine. I love *Dragon Magic*!"

Dr. Venus Ann Maher

"Jan Ögren's stories brought much joy to me ... almost as if I was going back to my precious childhood, when I was surrounded by enchanting and fun stories that also had so much meaning and a strong moral element. All of Jan's beautiful and thoughtful stories contain great positive messages that I truly appreciate. Her writing style is fun, playful, adventurous, creative, and filled with important life lessons. These stories also fill me with a great sense of wonder and curiosity that reminds me to keep my childlike spirit alive.

The stories in section three about the stories gave me insight into the writer's experiences and the inspirations that helped create "The Hungry Ghost" and "Butterfly Girl." I grew very fond of the characters, and loved being immersed in the beautiful nature descriptions: great stuff!"

Vickie Rodriguez

Other books by Jan Ögren

———— ✦ ————

Dividing Worlds

Mundos em Divisao: Uma Parabola Para Nossos Tempos
Barany Publisher
Sao Paulo, Brazil

Weaving the Web: Amazing Fables for All Ages Vol. 2
(Forthcoming from Namen Press, 2016)

DRAGON MAGIC
Amazing Fables for All Ages

enjoy,

Jan ☺

Jan Ögren

DRAGON MAGIC: AMAZING FABLES FOR ALL AGES

ISBN-13: 978-0692362556
ISBN-10: 069236255X

First Printing, 2015
First Edition, 2015

Editor: Madeleine Fahrenwald
Cover art: Justin Adams
Illustrations: Scott Fray
Design: Cris Wanzer

www.JanOgren.net

Published by Namen Press
NamenPress@gmail.com

Namen Press

Dedication

To my mother
Marjorie Jean Ogren
(1920-2013)

Not only did she introduce me to storytelling,
she was the biggest fan of my stories.
She reread them often, and always
encouraged me in my writing.

Contents

———— ✦ ————

Acknowledgments

I consider writing a group effort. Alone I can create stories I like and understand. But to share the stories with others, I need a village of readers and listeners. It's the group effort that transforms them from personal stories into mythic fables.

First, I want to acknowledge the source of many of the fables: the Circle of Grandmother and Grandfather Story Tellers. I also want to thank the animals, trees, and other spirits who shared their stories with me.

I am incredibly grateful to Dr. Ruth-Inge Heinze and all the organizers, fellow presenters, and participants at the International Conference on the Study of Shamanism and Alternative Modes of Healing from 1990 to 2014. Presenting at that conference launched me in the direction of being a storyteller and now an author. Without all of their encouragement, this book would definitely not exist. (The full story of Ruth-Inge's central role in inspiring this book, and how I met the Circle of Grandmother and Grandfather Story Tellers, is in section four: "Magical Worlds, Magical Stories.")

I appreciate my wonderful parents for being so supportive and proud of me, and for having faith in me for all these years. My mother, Marjorie Jean Ogren, who gave me a love of stories and constantly asked me when my next book was coming out. My father, Ken Ogren, who carefully read and edited all the stories *twice*.

Special thanks to my god-daughter Zory Wilson and her mother Pat Wilson for giving me a seven-year-old's perspective on these stories back in 2005. I loved hearing Zory's interpretation of the "moral" of each story and how painstakingly Pat checked all the words, circling each one that Zory had trouble understanding.

I couldn't have finished this book without my "writing sister" and good friend, Venus Maher, who helped me through the many, many, many hours of rewrites. She kept me on course and made the process fun!

To all my readers at various stages: your comments were invaluable. Writing is like having to get dressed up for an important event with NO mirrors. Your reflections and insights were vital as I tried on different words and sentences, asking over and over, "Does this work? How does this look?" Without the honesty and constant feedback from my incredible group of readers, *Dragon Magic* wouldn't be dressed up and ready to meet the world.

Much gratitude to: Andrea Selieta Williamson, Angela Lam, Cassandra Vieten, Dale Jenkins, Dean Watson, Dianna L. Grayer, Kate Sorensen, Ken Ogren, Kitty Wells, Lisa Beytia, Lucy Lewis, Marjorie Ogren, Pat Wilson, Sheridan Gold, Shelley Stewart, MSW, Rev. Shirley Ranck, Dr. Venus Maher, Vickie Rodriguez, and Zory Wilson.

Thank you to all the people – especially the children – who have listened for over twenty years as I have told and adapted these stories. Your bright eyes, smiles, and exclamations of wonder and surprise gave me invaluable feedback. Your excitement encouraged me to keep telling the stories and gave me the determination to gather them all together in this book.

Skinner House Press helped me believe in myself as an author when this collection was almost published as: *How the Dragons Became Extinct and Other Tales* in 2005. I incorporated their suggestion to share a few of the stories about how I received the fables into this book.

Special acknowledgments go to: my partner Dean Watson, for all your support as I've run off to writing retreats and stayed up late writing – and for putting up with getting second billing in my author bio to our annoyingly intelligent cat. Our cat SheBe, for giving me the most popular sentence I ever wrote (see my bio at the end of the book). Our new cat Esprit, for all the purring and lap-time he performed while trying to distract me from writing.

Stanley Krippner, for being an amazing listener and supporter. Glenn Hartelius for transcribing "First Solstice" when I was trying to make the transition from oral storyteller to writer, and for introducing the character of "Little Fir." Brenda Phillips, for encouraging me to make this the best book possible. Bobbie and Bill, for making their beautiful home by the ocean available for writing retreats with my writing sister Venus. Redwood Writers, a Branch of California Writers Club, for being such a supportive organization.

The numerous Unitarian Universalist congregations that gave me the opportunity to share the stories during services with both children and adults.

Especially to the Unitarian Universalist Congregations in Santa Rosa and Petaluma, California.

I so appreciate the continued support I receive from the spirit world, above all the practical editing by Grandmother Evelyn Eaton, who used to be an author when she walked in this physical world, as well as the assistance I've gotten from all the spirits who helped connect me with the right people in order to birth this book and send it out into the world.

Thanks to Justin Adams for his vision of the front cover; and for being an amazing artist who was willing to step into a new genre to create this gorgeous cover art. To Scott Fray, who did the illustrations for two stories 20 years ago, and who reappeared in my life to create more fabulous illustrations for this book. To Madeleine Fahrenwald for her editing, especially for rearranging words to adjust for my tendency to use French sentence structure; and for suggesting edits and additions so appropriate that I thought I'd written them myself. And finally, thanks to Cris Wanzer of Book and Manuscript Services for showing up in my life at exactly the right time to birth this book.

Section One

---✦---

Introduction

✦

Once upon a time I was a little girl who loved to hear stories. My mother would share an adventure from another world with me almost every night before I went to sleep. I was very lucky, because my mother was a storyteller who shared her tales at libraries and schools. Wherever she told stories, I would go with her. I listened to her tell them over and over again. I listened so much that I began to know the stories myself and was able to tell them to my friends.

As a young girl, I was an explorer. Some of my travels were in my backyard or at a nearby stream, but many of them were through the pages of books. When I was older, I had to respond to teachers' questions about what I was reading. Often I understood it one way, while they expected me to see it a different way. Sometimes I was more interested in the characters I was supposed to hate, and bored by the heroes. Other times, I would change the ending in my mind if I didn't think it was the right one. If I really liked the characters, I used them to create my own story. It didn't help me earn good grades in my English classes, but it filled my life with fantasy, friends, and adventure.

Nature was an abundant source of material for my imagination. I would sit very quietly by an anthill behind my house, and the scurrying of the tiny insects welcomed me into their world. I got a sense of how enormous a tiny twig is when you have to crawl over it, and how moving thousands of grains of sand one by one up and out of the ground creates a tunnel and more room for ant-size possibilities. I could hear the wind talking to the trees above me and the bushes sighing their response. I knew the wisest creature in my backyard world was the old toad who lived in a tree with a cave at its base. All that made more sense to me than why I should put the fork on the left side of the plate, or why the dishes had to be washed before being put in the dishwasher.

Not only was the natural world easier to understand than the people-world, everyone in it had a message for me. The butterflies building their cocoons, the grass tickling my feet, the clouds waving in the sky, they all wanted to talk with me and share their tales. The world was alive with many voices. But I noticed, especially as I grew older, that no one else seemed to hear them.

I was scared of how different I seemed to be until, in my early twenties, I met someone who heard and was aware of even more messages than me. His name was Red Eagle, and he was a Mescalero Apache Medicine Man. The Mescalero Apache are a Native American tribe in the southwest. A Medicine Man or Woman helps the community with healing and special ceremonies by connecting with the universe beyond our physical world and listening to the subtle voices of our Mother Earth. Red Eagle didn't think it strange that I talked to grasshoppers or heard stories in the wind. His ancestors had been listening to these voices for generations upon generations.

For the first time I didn't feel so alone in the human world. In the tradition of his people, Red Eagle adopted me into his family and I became his daughter, his friend, and his apprentice. He explained that everything was full of life and that everything was interconnected. We'd laugh together when I'd get confused by trying to divide the world into separate parts: material or spiritual, mind or body, natural or human. Or when I'd try to make a hierarchy where some types of life were more important than others. He saw things in circles, as Coyote learns to do in the story "The First Medicine Circle."

With his encouragement I listened even more closely to messages from all sources: books, trees, people, animals, birds, and more. When I had trouble dealing with someone or was facing a difficult challenge, a story would often come to help me better understand myself and the situation. That's what happened with the story of "The Hungry Ghost." Then stories began showing up to help others, like "The Butterfly Girl" and "Cat's Gift."

In this book a dinosaur's life is completely changed by an earthquake, the dragons discover that they are becoming invisible, and evergreen trees must deal with the sun disappearing from the sky. The characters in the stories all face different challenges. What does a tadpole do if he doesn't want to grow up to be a frog? What happens when children see things that adults don't believe are real? How does a blind bunny find friends? As these people, animals, and plants shared their challenges with me, I learned how to face my own struggles and find answers for myself.

At first, the stories came to me more as feelings and a sense of something happening. Then they started emerging as full narratives like the ones my mother used to tell. Now when Frog offers to tell me a story, I'm able to hear him in a way that allows me to convey his adventure directly through words and eventually onto paper.

✦

The first section of this book contains the introduction. Section two is a theme index, which has suggestions on what stories you can use for different life situations and will help you locate a special story to help a child, adult, or group deal with specific challenges. Section three contains twelve fables, followed by section four where I share real life tales about how I received four of the stories and who told them to me. In these tales I share more about my experiences apprenticing with Red Eagle and my first meeting with a dragon.

✦

This book is a collection of living stories. Don't expect to hear the same thing every time you read or tell them. The sources of these stories are alive and in our world today, speaking through these fables and weaving their messages into our lives. They don't have to be read in order. Listen for which ones call to you and share them with others, especially with children too young to read all the words themselves.

Jan Ögren, MFT 2014

Section Two

———— ✦ ————

Theme Index

This section offers a list of stories according to themes. You can use it to find a special story to help a child, adult, or group deal with specific challenges.

———————— ✦ ————————

Abundance and Gratitude: *Change Wizard, Hungry Ghost, Medicine Circle, Solstice*

Self-**Acceptance:** *Anna, Dragon Magic, Frogs & Wishes*

Accepting others: *Anna, Blind Bunny, Cat's Gift, Dragon Magic*

Transforming **Black and White** thinking: *Blind Bunny, Change Wizard, Medicine Circle, Solstice, Yin and Yang*

Dealing with **Bullying:** *Anna, Cat's Gift, Frogs & Wishes*

Challenge, Change and Adversity: *Dragon Magic, Frogs & Wishes, Magical Quakes, Medicine Circle, Solstice*

Co-dependence: *Blind Bunny*

Competition and sibling rivalry: *Anna, Hungry Ghost, Magical Quakes*

Courage and Determination: *Butterfly Girl, Frogs & Wishes, Solstice*

Feeling **Different:** *Anna, Blind Bunny, Dragon Magic, Frogs & Wishes*

Death and Loss: *Cat's Gift, Magical Quakes, Solstice*

Disappointment: *Butterfly Girl, Cat's Gift, Medicine Circle*

Going beyond **Duality**: *Solstice, Yin and Yang*

Embarrassment and Shame: *Anna, Cat's Gift*

Encouraging **Exploration** and Discovery: *Butterfly Girl, Magical Quakes, Medicine Circle, Solstice, Yin and Yang*

Faith and trust: *Butterfly Girl, Dragon Magic, Solstice*

Fears: *Dragon Magic, Magical Quakes, Solstice*

Listening to **Feelings:** *Anna, Blind Bunny, Butterfly Girl, Frogs & Wishes*

Friendship: *Anna, Blind Bunny, Cat's Gift, Hungry Ghost*

Greed and Scarcity: *Change Wizard, Hungry Ghost*

Guides and spirit helpers: *Anna, Butterfly Girl, Cat's Gift*

Hope: *Butterfly Girl, Solstice*

Learning to **Let Go:** *Change Wizard, Magical Quakes, Solstice*

Loneliness and feeling Alone: *Blind Bunny, Cat's Gift*

Money and Consumerism: *Change Wizard, Hungry Ghost, Magical Quakes,*

Connecting with **Nature:** *Blind Bunny, Butterfly Girl, Solstice, Yin & Yang*

Patience and Faith: *Butterfly Girl, Magical Quakes, Solstice*

Perfectionism: *Cat's Gift, Change Wizard*

Problem Solving: *Anna, Cat's Gift, Magical Quakes, Medicine Circle, Yin and Yang*

Rejection: *Anna, Cat's Gift, Dragon Magic, Frogs & Wishes,*

Respect: *Cat's Gift, Dragon Magic,*

Self-Esteem: *Anna, Frogs & Wishes*

Sharing: *Change Wizard, Hungry Ghost*

Social Responsibility, class and race issues: *Blind Bunny, Change Wizard, Dragon Magic, Frogs & Wishes, Hungry Ghost*

Discovering hidden **Talents** and Gifts: *Anna, Dragon Magic, Frogs & Wishes, Magical Quakes, Medicine Circle*

Transgender: *Frogs & Wishes*

Transitions and Moving: *Blind Bunny, Dragon Magic, Magical Quakes, Medicine Circle*

Trusting yourself: *Anna, Butterfly Girl, Frogs & Wishes*

Section Three

◆

Amazing Fables for All Ages

The Butterfly Girl

✦

There once was a little girl named Ella who loved to visit her grandparents in the country. They had a cozy house with a garden in back surrounded by woods. Ella enjoyed spending her afternoons looking at the plants and watching the creatures of the garden. Her grandpa often sat with her telling her the names of the birds, what they ate, and what flowers and trees they liked. He taught her how to water the plants, how to pinch back the old flowers to keep the plants blooming, and the best way to pick vegetables. When Ella found an odd-looking bug, Grandpa always knew what it was called and what its job was in the garden.

Ella liked the flowers, the birds, and all the good things to eat. But best of all she loved the butterflies. They flew through the garden on the most delicate of wings, which allowed them to walk along the edge of a flower petal without squishing it. Then they'd slip their long tongues into the center of each fragrant blossom to drink its sweetness.

One day as they were sitting next to the camellia bush watching a brown striped caterpillar chew on a leaf, Ella asked, "Grandpa, what's it like to be a butterfly?"

"That's a good question," he replied. "Let me get my books and I'll show you." He went inside and brought out four thick books filled with drawings and photographs. Together they searched for all the pictures of caterpillars, cocoons, and butterflies. After he'd read her everything he could find about butterflies, Ella sat next to him twirling a tiny stick between her fingers, thinking very hard. Finally she said, "I liked learning all those neat facts, and the pictures were really nice. But Grandpa, I want to know what it's like to *be* a butterfly!"

"What's it like? Well, umm, hmmm," he said, crinkling his nose and squinting his eyes as though he were trying to see an answer on the ground in front of him. "I know a way to find out!" he exclaimed, standing up quickly. Ella jumped up, ready to follow her grandpa, because he could always find the answer for any question.

Around the side of the house they went. Past the woodpile and into the old storage shed. "Let's see what we can find in here," said Grandpa. After moving a lot of boxes, disturbing three lizards and many spiders, he let out a cheer. "Here it is! I knew we still had it somewhere."

"What is it, Grandpa?" asked Ella, looking at a very dirty and cracked old fish tank.

"This is going to be a future home for butterflies!" he said, dusting off the tank. "Grab that old mesh screen behind you."

Ella looked around and saw the bent screen her grandpa had taken off the kitchen window last year. "This one?"

"Yep, that'll be perfect." He tore the metal frame off until just the mesh was left. Then they took the tank, the mesh, and some string and went out into the garden. First they filled the bottom with dirt, then they added twigs and leaves. "Now we go caterpillar-hunting," Grandpa told Ella. They found lots of yellow and green ones, two with black spots and a very hairy orange one. Grandpa helped Ella place them on the sticks. Then he put the wire mesh over the top and secured it with the string so the caterpillars couldn't climb out. When they were finished, they put it in a corner of the back porch. "All you have to do is keep it filled with tasty leaves, watch it closely, and soon you'll learn what it's like to be a butterfly," Grandpa explained.

Ella checked it every day, while the caterpillars ate and ate and ate. After a few weeks, one by one, they all built cocoons. Then it was really boring, because nothing happened for a long time. Grandpa decided to cut one of them open to show Ella what was inside. At first she was curious, but all they found were strange parts of a half-caterpillar, half-butterfly, and lots of yucky mushy stuff. Then she was very sad, because that caterpillar would never get to learn what it was like to be a butterfly. She thought that was Grandpa's worst idea ever.

One day, when the flowers had been blooming for many weeks, Ella was passing by the back porch when she noticed movement in the old fish tank. A cocoon was shaking and quivering. "Grandpa, Grandpa! Come see what the caterpillars are doing," Ella yelled as she raced back into the house.

"Those aren't caterpillars anymore," Grandpa said, as he joined her on the porch. Then he took the top off the tank and carried it to the garden. Ella and her grandpa watched as one of the cocoons opened and a beautiful orange butterfly emerged. It clung delicately to its old home, opening and closing its wings in the sun. With a little spring it launched itself into the air, followed by Ella who ran behind. She jumped in circles on the ground as the butterfly flew back and forth among the flowers and trees. Over the next three days many different butterflies emerged, striped and dotted in browns, oranges, reds, and yellows. They were dressed in all the colors of the flowers and the earth. After the last one had come out of its cocoon and Ella had danced around the yard with it, she walked slowly over to her grandpa. "Grandpa, that was fun watching them come out of the cocoons. But I still don't know what it's like to *be* a butterfly."

Grandpa drummed his fingers against his chin as he thought very hard. "I'm sorry Ella, I don't know any other ways to explain to you about butterflies. We've gone through all my books and you got to see how they're born. I don't know what else there is to teach you."

Ella walked away and sat down by the woods to stare at the butterflies dancing with the flowers. The summer continued, with birds to watch and vegetables to eat. Sometimes Ella saw a butterfly she was sure she had witnessed being born. It would fly around the garden enjoying the daisies and daffodils.

Fall came, school started, and she spent less time in her grandparents' garden. Then one Saturday near the end of October, her grandparents took her into town to get a costume for Halloween. As they walked down the sidewalk trying to decide which store to go into first, they passed a second-hand store they had never noticed before. In the center of the display window was a shimmering butterfly costume. The body and wings were all shades of yellow and orange, and it had black tights to go with it.

"That's my costume! I want that one!" Ella shouted, bouncing up and down in front of the store. It was exactly her size, so they bought it for her. As soon as they got home, Ella pulled the costume over her head and slipped her legs into the tights. There were fluffy pink antennae sticking up out of a thin crown that she fastened on the top of her head. Then her grandmother helped her slip the wings over her shoulders and attach them to her back. Ella wiggled her shoulders and swung her head around until everything felt just right. Then she went outside and ran around the garden, jumping and hopping and smelling flowers. Her grandparents got so tired from watching her that they had to sit down. As her circles around the yard grew smaller and smaller, Grandpa called out to her, "Hey, there's the prettiest butterfly I've seen all year! Now do you know what it's like to be a butterfly?"

Ella stared out into the woods beyond the garden for a few moments. She wanted to agree and say, "Yes, I know *just* what it's like to *be* a butterfly." She almost said it, but instead she looked her grandpa straight in the eye and said, "Grandpa, I know a lot about what it's like to be a girl running about in a butterfly costume, but no, I don't know what it's like to really *be* a butterfly."

They all stood there for a moment, and then her grandma nodded at her and went inside. There was something about the way her grandma looked at her that made Ella run after her calling, "Grandma, Grandma! Do you know how I could find out what it's like to *be* a butterfly?" Grandma sat down at the kitchen table and stared at a picture of her own grandmother that was hanging on the wall. It was a faded brown photo of a tall old woman standing next to a tree with a deer sniffing her outstretched hand. Ella glanced at the picture, then turned and saw the smile on her grandma's face. "You do! You do!" she sang as she danced around the table. "You know how I can find out what it's like to *be* a butterfly."

"Yes, I do," Grandma agreed. "But it's not going to be easy. What you are asking for is to see and feel the world as if you were something else. It's hard enough understanding how other people see the world, let alone a flying butterfly! It's not something you can read about or observe or even pretend…."

"I know, Grandma. I tried all those other ways. It did teach me some things, and some of it was really fun. But it didn't teach me what I really want to know."

Grandma paused until Ella was quiet and listening again. "It will take time and a lot of patience, so I want you to think about it. If you decide you really, truly in your heart want to know, then I do know a way you can learn it. But you'll have to do exactly what I say. And even then, you won't know until spring."

"Oh yes, Grandma, I want to know. I'll do everything you say. If I do a good job, can you show me by Thanksgiving?"

Grandma just smiled at her and said, "It's not about showing you. It's helping you to learn in a different way. I want you to think about it for three days first. Then, if you still want to know what it's like to *be* a butterfly, I'll help you."

She stood up and started to prepare dinner, as Ella pleaded, "But Grandma, I already know. I've known all summer. Please, please, can't I start now?"

Grandma handed her a bowl full of peas in the pods. "Shell these and we'll have them tonight with some basil and thyme from the garden." Ella chewed on her lower lip and tried not to say anything else about butterflies while she helped her grandma with dinner.

Three days later she ran to her grandparents' house after school and told her Grandma, "Yes. I want to know what it's like to *be* a butterfly. I'll do whatever you tell me."

"Okay, I can tell you really want to know. I'll help you, but we can only do it in the spring when it's butterfly time," Grandma told her.

Ella thought that winter was the longest one ever. Every time she tried to get her grandmother to talk about butterflies, she'd look outside and say, "It isn't that time of year yet, just think about caterpillars for now."

When the weather finally warmed up, Ella announced to Grandma, "I saw a caterpillar today. Can you teach me how to *be* a butterfly now?"

"Well," Grandma replied, "that's a sure sign of spring coming if I ever heard one. If you're going to learn to *be* a butterfly, you'd better do what the caterpillars are doing now."

"They're eating all the new leaves off the azalea bush you love so much."

"Little girls don't need to eat that kinda stuff, but you've got the right idea. It's time to eat and drink a lot," Grandma said. Then she quickly walked outside to see if she could convince the caterpillars to eat another plant instead of her favorite flowering bush.

For the next month Ella ate and drank everything her grandma gave her. She also watched caterpillars, just in case there was anything else they were doing that was important, but all they seemed to do was eat.

Then very early one Saturday morning, when Ella sat down at the breakfast table, she noticed that there was nothing there: no juice, no fruit, no cereal or toast, not even a muffin. Grandma patted her gently on the shoulder and said, "Go up to your room and put on your most comfortable clothes. Bring a warm sweater too." When Ella came down they went out to the garden together. There was a mist floating just above the ground as the air slowly began to warm with the new day. Grandma led her to the edge of the woods where there was an assortment of cardboard, blankets, and plastic sheets her grandparents used to cover the vegetables when it got too cold at night. They sat down near the pile and Grandma explained how Ella could use all these things to build a nest big enough to crawl into. She finished by saying, "To know what it's like to *be* a butterfly, you have to build a cocoon for yourself and stay in it until the answer comes to you. Do you still want to do it?"

"You mean I'll have no food or water? And I can't get out and play at all?"

"Yes, you got it. No food or water. And NO going out to play."

"What if I need to pee?"

"That's ok. You can come out for that. But nothing else."

"But Grandma, it took weeks and weeks for the caterpillars to change!" Ella said, remembering how she had watched them last year.

"Well, for little girls it usually takes one day and one night. I won't think badly of you if you decide not to do it. I'll still love you and be proud of you just the same. It's your choice."

Ella bit her lower lip and tried to quiet the uneasiness stirring in her stomach. "I want to do it."

So with Grandma's help, Ella built herself a cocoon. The blankets made a soft, warm nest with the cardboard forming the sides and top, and over it all they draped the plastic to protect her from the nighttime dew. While they were working on it, Grandpa came by asking questions. "Shouldn't she take some water in at least? Won't she be too cold at night? What if she gets scared?" He kept talking on and on as the two of them worked. He walked away shaking his head after they crawled underneath the cardboard together to try to arrange the blankets so there would be a little room to squirm around in.

Just as the sun started to peek above the trees, they finished the cocoon. Then it was time for Ella to climb in. Her grandma closed up the entrance, reminding her once more, "If you have to come out before one day and one night are finished, I won't think badly of you."

The first hour passed quickly. Then the second hour took longer. By the eighth hour, Ella decided she knew exactly what a caterpillar feels like while it's waiting to be a butterfly. It was very boring, a little scary, and she got very thirsty and hungry. By the time the sun was setting and it was getting colder, Ella wanted to crawl out very badly, but Grandma had said that if she emerged too soon, she'd have to wait until next spring to try again. So Ella huddled in her small dim cocoon waiting for something to happen.

As it got darker and darker, the noises from the crickets and bugs got louder and louder. The birds began to sing even though it was nighttime. They all seemed to be saying, "Come out, come out." Their voices were coming from the top of her cocoon, not the bottom where the opening was. As Ella squirmed up to try to hear better, she noticed that there was a lot of room near the top.

Why didn't I use this space before? I wouldn't have felt so squished all those hours waiting in here, Ella thought as she kept crawling.

There seemed to be a light up there too. As she crept toward it, it got brighter and the sounds got louder. Soon she found herself in a circle of crickets, birds, and bugs. There was even a fluffy owl. They were all dancing around a gathering of fireflies so bright it looked like a fire burning in the middle of their circle. When they saw Ella they crowded around her, urging her to join them. As she danced with them, she bounced up into the air. With every jump she stayed airborne a little bit longer. Then she was floating in the sky. Looking behind her, she saw huge yellow and orange things attached to her back. She was so surprised she stopped flapping them and she drifted back to earth. She stood up on her six thin legs and twisted around to look over her shoulder. There they were: big, beautiful, butterfly wings coming out of her back, just like the costume. But now she had an extra muscle extending from her shoulder blades down the center of her back that made her wings open and close. Ella gently rose back into the air. She felt connected to everything: the other insects, the trees, the rocks. She could even taste the air and knew there would be rain the next day. Looking around, she saw all the creatures and plants as her friends. Some might eat her as a butterfly, and some she might eat, but not tonight, because they were all celebrating together. Ella danced in the air, fluttering around and around the circle.

In the morning she squirmed out of the cocoon. She crawled out the bottom where she had come in a day ago. The top looked small, just like it did when she and her grandmother had built it. She slowly unbent until she was standing tall and straight by the time her grandparents came over to her.

"Well," her grandpa asked, "do you know what it's like to be a butterfly now?"

Ella looked up at them. "Yes, Grandpa, I know."

"Tell us: what's it like?"

"It's well, um, ah, um," Ella tried to say. "It's just like . . . Well, you know it's kinda like. . .um."

"You mean you didn't find out?" Grandpa asked. "All that work and time and you still don't know?"

"I know. I do know," said Ella. "I *was* a butterfly."

"So tell us: what was it like?" he asked again.

"Being a butterfly is just like . . . well, it tastes of dew . . . I mean, it's . . .floaty and. . . ." Ella frowned and tried again. "I'm sure it's, it's . . . maybe kind of. . . ." She moved her arms and waved her hands at them, but the words didn't come. "I can't explain it!" Ella said, with tears in her eyes.

Grandma knelt down beside her. "That's all right, Ella. Some things just can't be said in words. After all, butterflies don't talk in words, do they?" Ella shook her head. "And you do know *inside* how it feels to *be* a butterfly, don't you?" Ella nodded. "Just because you can't explain it doesn't mean your experience wasn't real." Ella nodded again, a grin starting to spread across her face as she remembered the feeling of being a butterfly.

Grandpa sat down next to them. "I understand," he said. "There are some things you learn in books, and some things you understand by watching. Pretending is a good way to discover things too. But when you want to *know* what something *feels like,* it helps to learn through experience. So instead of trying to explain it with words, why don't you show us, in your own way, what it's like to *be* a butterfly?"

"I can do that," Ella agreed, nodding her head. Her grandparents got comfortable on the ground, with their backs against a tall tree, while Ella walked a few feet away. First she reached to the ground as though she was eating armfuls of grass and leaves. Then she hugged herself tight and knelt on the ground, covering her head with her hands. She stayed still a long time, then her grandparents heard her humming. As the sound grew louder, her arms started to lift. Her head rose slowly, with her eyes tightly shut, and an expression of pure joy on her face. Her hands floated higher, pulling her whole body up. She started to twirl, dipping and fluttering her arms. She was humming loudly now and her arm-wings pulsed with the sound.

Her grandparents looked on in awe as she circled the garden. After the third time around she came back and stood in front of them. "Can you tell now, Grandpa, that I *know* what it's like to *be* a butterfly?" Ella asked.

"Yes, I certainly can," he agreed. "You also showed me how you can't put that kind of knowing into simple words."

Grandma looked up at Ella and said, "Not only do you know what it's like to *be* a butterfly, you've also learned that if you want to know something, you can always find a way to explore it." Then she smiled at her granddaughter. "Even though sometimes the way you learn it is kind of strange and magical."

"Yes, that's true," said Ella, thinking of the circle of creatures she'd danced with. Then her stomach rumbled. "And I discovered something else, too."

"What?" they asked her.

"When you lie in a cocoon for a day and a night without food or water, you get hungry. Can I have something to eat now?"

"Certainly," Grandpa said. "In fact, we fixed your favorite breakfast to honor all the effort you put into learning what it's like to *be* a butterfly. Come on," he said, standing up and holding out his hands to both of them. "Let's go!" And they all walked into the kitchen together.

Frogs, Fishes, and Wishes

✦

In a little pond crowded with tadpoles lived a brownish-green one named Marvis. It was a wonderfully slimy place with lots to eat and nice layers of ooze to hide in. Marvis loved to swim in the pond and feel the flow of wetness along his body. He couldn't wait to develop gills, fins, and a strong, thin tail so he could swim deeper and farther through the water.

One day when he was practicing his swimming, one of his thousands of cousins started shouting excitedly from the far side of the pond.

"Hey, Marvis," called Freddy. "Look here! Look at what I'm growing!"

Marvis swam over eagerly, thinking that Freddy must be developing his gills. But when he looked, all he saw were two bumps halfway down Freddy's tail. "What are those?"Marvis asked.

"The beginnings of my legs!" Freddy cried happily.

"Legs!"Marvis exclaimed in horror. "You poor thing! They'll slow you down when you're swimming. I hope they don't grow any larger."

"What do you mean?" asked Freddy. "Legs are what we'll need to be able to hop around."

"Just think," added Jumit as she came up to admire Freddy's leg-buds, "soon you'll be able to crawl onto the land."

"Look!" cried Rogens, another of his many cousins. "Here comes a frog." They all turned to watch as the frog swam by. He went straight to the bank and then clambered up onto a pile of wet leaves on the edge.

"Oh, isn't he marvelous!" Jumit exclaimed. "I can't wait until I can do that."

"Why would you want to go onto that awful hard ground?" Marvis asked. "The water is so friendly and fun to move around in. I can't wait to grow up to be a fish and go exploring."

"But, Marvis," Freddy said. "We're all going to become frogs, and frogs hop on the land and live in the mud near the pond."

"I'm going to be a fish," insisted Marvis.

"Don't be silly," Rogens said. "You're a tadpole and then you'll become a frog. That's just the way it is and that's the way it's always been. All tadpoles grow up to eat bugs and hop around on the land."

Marvis didn't like being called silly, and he didn't like the idea of eating bugs. He knew he was meant to be a fish. So while all the others watched the frogs and imagined themselves hopping around on solid ground, Marvis dreamed of swimming and finding larger and larger ponds, or maybe even a lake. Someday he hoped to find a river that would lead to the ocean. His secret wish was not only to swim, but also to fly like the birds overhead. But that seemed too much to hope for, so he concentrated on growing up to be a fish.

Soon Marvis also started growing leg-buds on either side of his tail. He tried to ignore the bothersome bulges, but soon they were interfering with his swimming. As they grew, he squeezed them tightly against his tail so he wouldn't notice them as much. Then, to his dismay, his tail started to feel loose, and one day it fell right off.

"Freddy," Marvis cried. "Look what happened to my tail!"

"What luck!" responded Freddy. "I hope mine drops off soon."

"But how will I swim?" Marvis asked.

"Frogs don't need to do that much swimming. And look at how long and strong your legs are now," Freddy told him.

"How did you get your tail to fall off so quickly?" asked Jumit, swimming over to them. "I'd been noticing that you kept your legs tightly pressed alongside your tail. Is that what helped you get rid of it so fast?"

"I didn't want to get rid of my tail!" Marvis wailed. "How will I ever swim to the lakes and streams? I'll never make it to the ocean now."

"What's wrong with stupid Marvis?" asked Rogens, paddling over from near the bank where he had been practicing kicking his legs. "He's not still talking about becoming a fish, is he?"

"He's just shocked at losing his tail so fast," Freddy answered. "He's the first one, so he feels a little different right now. But we'll all be losing those silly things soon."

As Freddy, Rogens, and Jumit all talked about the fastest way to get their tails to drop off, Marvis swam clumsily away. He wondered if Jumit was right. Maybe pushing his legs against his tail for so long had made it drop off. *Well,* he thought to himself. *If it was the fault of my legs, then they'll just have to take the place of my beautiful tail.* He splashed over to the bank, careful to not touch the muddy side, and grabbed a long blade of grass growing in the water. He used his mouth and his small front legs to twist it around to form a strong, thin rope. Then he reached down and tied his feet together so that his two legs became one long, slightly bumpy tail. He pushed himself off from the shore and his legs now moved together, propelling him through the water. *That's better!* Then he sighed and thought, *But I do miss my fish-like tail!*

Over the next few weeks, hundreds and thousands of his cousins lost their tails and began exploring the sticky mud near the banks, and then harder things like leaves, rocks, and sticks. But Marvis remained swimming in the water. He had to work very hard because his hind end was getting larger and heavier as his legs continued to grow. He tried swimming with the fish in the deeper part of the pond, but he had to keep coming up for air. Sometimes he paddled over toward the bank and held onto a floating stick to rest for a while. Then he would stare longingly up at the birds and dream of being a creature that could both fly and swim. If he floated too near where his cousins were practicing their hopping, Rogens would start calling him "no-legs," "water-boy," and "Marvis the Tail." Before the others could join Rogens in taunting him, Marvis would swim back to the deeper places, away from where the young frogs were playing.

One day, after it had been raining for weeks, the water level in the pond rose so high that it connected to a larger pool. Marvis quickly swam over to explore this new place. He found a stream flowing from the far end of that pond that led to a lake. At the end of the lake he discovered a river. Following the river for many days, he eventually reached a bay, and there at last he could taste the salt of the nearby ocean. Here there were no tadpoles or frogs to tease him and tell him he had to be a frog. He practiced diving and swimming in the calm bay, preparing for the day when he would journey to the wide-open ocean. Once in a while when he got tired, he hung on to a floating log. But mostly he swam and swam. "Now I'm finally the fish I always wished to be," Marvis sang happily, as he dove through a school of fish.

"Nope!" said one of the fish as he passed.

"What do you mean?" asked Marvis, turning around to look at the large salmon that had spoken to him.

"Nope, not a fish," said the salmon. "Not sure what you are, but you're not a fish."

"I am too!" cried Marvis. "Can't you see how well I can swim?"

"Well, you do swim pretty well. . . . Odd-looking tail, though," the salmon remarked, while slowly swimming in circles around Marvis. Marvis wished he would hurry up and leave, because he needed to swim up to the surface to breathe and he didn't want to do that in front of the salmon.

By now there were several fish staring at him. "Excuse me," Marvis finally said, as he swished up to the surface to suck in some air. He came right back down, but all the fish were gone. After that experience, Marvis tried to ignore the fish. He loved living in the bay, though he did miss Freddy and Jumit, but not Rogens.

One day a dark shape flashed past him in the water. It came from the surface and dove straight down through the water. When it came back up, it settled on the surface, floating calmly there. Marvis thought he was the only one who could both dive down deep and rest on the surface of the water. He was curious, so he swam over to this new creature.

"What are you?" asked Marvis.

"I'm a cormorant, and my name is Chorton," the creature replied. "Cormorants are a type of water bird."

"My name's Marvis. What's a water bird?"

"I'm a bird that can fly in the sky and swim under the water."

"You can? That's wonderful!" Marvis said. "Why were you diving so deep?"

"Looking for fish. I eat fish." Chorton said. "But I don't see very well, so I'm not very good at finding fish."

"Oh," said Marvis, feeling uncomfortable. "Do you eat frogs too?"

"No, I don't care much for frogs. I just like eating fish." Chorton turned and squinted at Marvis. "What are you?"

Marvis considered saying that he was a frog so Chorton wouldn't want to eat him. But then he thought to himself, *I would rather die as a fish than live as a frog!* So he told Chorton, "I'm a fish."

"My, what luck!" exclaimed the cormorant. He opened his beak wide and started moving toward Marvis.

"I'm a fish, I'm a fish, I'm a fish," Marvis repeated, as he watched Chorton's gaping mouth coming closer and closer. He could see the sharp edges on the inside of his beak and the opening at the back of his throat that led straight down into the bird's stomach. Then Chorton stopped and peered down at Marvis.

"What are you babbling about?" he asked.

"All my life I've believed I was a fish. Now, when you eat me, at last I'll really *be* a fish!"

Chorton turned his beak aside and moved his eye closer to get a better look at Marvis. "You mean you aren't really a fish?"

"Well actually, I was born a tadpole in a pond far away from here. The others said I had to become a frog. But I've always felt that I was a fish," Marvis told him.

"Oh dear, oh dear," exclaimed Chorton. "I almost ate a frog! Now that I look at you, I realize I made a mistake: I asked the wrong question. My apologies. Let me ask again. Who you do FEEL you are?"

Marvis started to say "A fish" but then he stopped. "Now that I've met you, I can admit it: I've always really wished to both fly like a bird and swim like a fish. I never even knew that was possible until this moment. But now that I see you, I know that's what feels right for me."

"Aha, now I see. You're another cormorant," Chorton said.

"Well, I want to . . . I mean, I feel I am . . . but . . . can I be?" Marvis stuttered.

"Of course. And your answer was just right. Do you know where you are?"

Marvis swished himself upward, poking his eyes up higher to see the bay and the shoreline in the distance.

"Oh, you can't see it with your eyes." Chorton explained. "Feel it inside and all around you."

Marvis floated, feeling a tingling of excitement throughout his whole being. He looked inside himself and it was like opening up a box filled with joy and hope. "The water is tickling me! It's like it wants me to do something."

The cormorant nodded his beak and squawked. "Yes, this is the Bay of Truth. When you speak what is really true, not what others tell you, or what you think you should say, but what is genuinely true inside you, it becomes real!"

"What do you mean?" Marvis felt the joy bursting through his skin. "Oh, please tell me quickly!"

"Just look down at your reflection in the water and you'll see who you are," Chorton advised.

Marvis started to look down, but he realized that his head was now high above the water. He wobbled, feeling like he was falling over, so he spread his wings to balance himself. "Wings!" he shouted. "I have wings!" He wanted to see his back, but he swung his head around so fast that he fell right into the water. He was able to twist and turn his new body so easily that soon he was bobbing beside Chorton again.

"What happened?" he asked. "How did I become a water bird?"

"But isn't that what you said you always knew you were?" asked Chorton, turning his head from side to side so he could examine Marvis, first with one eye and than the other.

"Well ... but ... how? I mean. . . ." Marvis stammered.

"You can become who you really are here, because this is the Bay of Truth. Isn't that why you journeyed to this bay?" Chorton asked.

"I always had the strongest wish to swim in the ocean. But I didn't know why." Now that Marvis was a bird and sat up higher on the water, he could see the ocean in the distance. He tried stretching up so he could see it even better, but that pushed his tail feathers too far into the water and he flopped over backwards.

Chorton kept talking, politely ignoring Marvis's splashing. "There are quite a few other cormorants in my flock who started out as tadpoles. Some even began as fish. I know a few who started as cormorants and then became frogs or fishes. You can't always tell just by looking at someone when they're young who they're going to become as they get older."

"Can I fly?" Marvis interrupted.

"I would certainly think so," Chorton said. "That is what a cormorant does, you know. Just stretch your neck out, paddle really hard like you're trying to run on top of the water, and flap your wings as fast as you can." Marvis did as Chorton told him and stumbled into the air. "Now tuck your feet up," Chorton directed as he flew beside Marvis, who was having a little trouble staying steady. "Now flatten your tail out. That's how you steer, you know. Watch out!" he cried, as Marvis almost bumped into him. "Don't move your tail so much: gentle, gentle. There you go. Much better. How's it feel now?"

"Marvelous!" cried Marvis. "I really am a water bird. Now I can swim and fly too!"

"And you have lots of friends," added Chorton. "Come on, I'll show you the flock and the trees where we nest."

Marvis flew close to Chorton, making sure his tail was steady so he wouldn't bump into him. "Thank you so much! If you hadn't come around, I would never have known I was really a cormorant."

"Happy to help out," said Chorton. "Frogs, fishes, or cormorants: you just gotta be who you know you are." Then the two cormorants sailed out to an island in the bay where hundreds of Chorton's cousins noisily squawked their welcome to Marvis.

Dragon Magic

✦

Once upon a time, on a mountainous island far, far away, there was an enormous cavern. It was cut deep into the side of a cliff, just above where the ocean waves crashed, and in it lived a family of dragons. Firzon, the oldest and largest of all the dragons, paced back and forth across the great council chamber near the mouth of the cavern. He was a fire-dragon, with golden wings and scales the color of the sun. His tail lashed to and fro as he strode across the gigantic room, scattering the boulders used for chairs by the dragons. They crashed into the walls and thundered down the hallways.

"Father!" cried Shimilis, running into the chamber. "What's wrong? Why are you so upset?"

But Firzon kept pacing. His daughter watched as he knocked several very comfortable rocks all the way out of the cave. She heard them crash into the ocean below. As his spiked tail thrashed across the floor Shimilis jumped into the air. Hovering in the middle of the great room, she yelled as loud as she could, "Father, what is the matter?"

Firzon stopped so fast his tail whipped behind him, denting the stone wall. "It's those humans!" he said. His huge diamond eyes stared out beyond the cavern rim, and flames danced along his white pointed teeth.

"What did they do?" his daughter asked.

"Nothing, Shim," he roared. "They did nothing at all!"

Shimilis waited, but her father just continued gazing out over the ocean. "I don't understand," she said. "What's wrong with doing nothing?"

Firzon strode over to his daughter, who drifted back to the floor now that it was safe to stand on it. "They're doing nothing!" her father hissed, blowing fire over Shim's head. "They don't notice us. They don't talk to us. They act as though we don't even exist! I sent Sirserpent with five other water-dragons to try to talk with them. I thought that if the humans were on the ocean in boats as big as we are, they might be more willing to talk to us. Sirserpent carefully approached them and called out a friendly greeting. And do you know what happened?" Firzon bellowed. Shimilis shook her scaly head. "The humans thought they were whales. Whales!" His great tail started lashing back and forth again, knocking more boulders over the edge and down into the ocean.

"How could they think the water-dragons were whales?" asked Shimilis. "Sirserpent has a very long neck and wings. Whales don't have wings. Did they try to explain who they were to the humans?"

"They tried," her father said, wrapping his tail around his body and crouching down on the cavern floor. "That's what's so sad. The dragons kept showing off their wings and how long their necks were, hoping the humans would see that they weren't whales. But it didn't work. The humans shot harpoons at them. They did the dragons no harm, of course, since they just bounced off their scales. Still, the indignity of it! Then the humans began yelling that the 'whales' disappeared beneath the sea and believed there was nothing in front of them. They even steered their boat right through one of the dragons!"

"What happened?"

Firzon sighed, filling the cavern with steam as a crystal tear rolled down his face. "It was too much for the dragon. First to be called a whale, then not to be seen at all. The confusion and despair was too much. She just dissolved into the ocean, becoming a million sparkling drops of water."

"Oh, no!" cried Shimilis, starting to cry crystal tears like her father. "What happened to the others?"

"Two more melted away, becoming part of the ocean again. The others got so weak that their wings started drooping. Luckily, some real whales came by and helped them get away from the humans before they also disappeared. Sirserpent and the other two are resting right now in the sea cavern below us." Shim's father turned to her and put his forepaw gently on her shoulder. "I've tried to keep you here to protect you, so you would never experience the agony of being ignored. It's the most terrible thing: to stand before another creature and have them look through you as though you didn't even exist. Or even worse, to have them think you are something else entirely and not see who you really are."

"But Father," Shimilis protested. "How is it that humans can't see us? I don't understand."

"They don't see us because they no longer believe in magic and magical creatures," Firzon said. Giant dragon-tears rolled out of his diamond eyes and pooled around his feet.

Shimilis backed up, staring at her father. "H...How can they not believe in magic?" she stammered.

"Oh, they used to," Firzon explained. "When you were born, many hundreds of years ago, all humans believed in magic. When we would fly over their villages, they would come out to watch us. They made statues of us and had parades that honored dragons. And there were human magicians who used to come and talk with us. They would bring us jewels, and we would share our knowledge and wisdom with them. Ahhhh," Firzon let out a long, slow sigh that filled the cavern with smoke. "I have not spoken with a human for a very long time. I don't even know if there are any wizards still alive today."

"Now I understand why you've wanted us to live so far away from the humans."

"I thought you would be safe here. This cavern can only be entered from the air or the ocean below. But every year there are more and more humans in the world. They keep exploring and expanding across the earth. I fear that some day they may even learn to fly."

"They won't be able to fly without magic, Father," Shim protested. "That's impossible."

"They're very clever. They're making new tools, weapons, and machines all the time. I have looked in the clearest of dragon crystals. I have seen that one day humans will be flying in metal machines in the air. But when I look into that future, I don't see dragons in the air. When I look across the land today, I see humans cutting down forests and building cities wherever they go." Firzon's head hung down low and he added, "I can no longer contact Erseth and her earth-dragon family. The humans were killing the trees where they lived, and she told me that she was going to try asking them to leave her home unharmed. But I haven't heard from her since then, and so I fear that she and all her tribes have melted into the earth."

"But what happened to them?" Shimilis shuddered, her scales rattling with fear.

Firzon swung his giant head close to his daughter and said quietly, "Because we are magic, we need to live in an enchanted world where *all* the creatures believe in magic – or else we will cease to exist. We will disappear into the water, the fire, the earth, or the air. I have heard of flocks of sky-dragons who flew over human cities. No one ran outdoors to look up and point into the sky. The people that did happen to gaze upward thought that the dragons were pretty clouds. All the magic drained out of the dragons, and they dissolved into the air."

"That's terrible, Father. Is there nothing we can do?"

"I've called a great council of all the remaining dragons. They'll be arriving here by the full moon. Together we will decide what to do. Perhaps there's another world where we can go, a land where all the creatures still believe in magic."

"But I don't want to leave this place. I love our home, with its steep mountains to fly over and the ocean to dive into," Shimilis protested, thinking about her favorite cliffs and the coves where she would lie in the warm sand.

"There's one possibility, but it will take all the dragons working together to try it," said Firzon. "I'll explain it to you at the meeting. Now can you please help me put all these boulders back, so we will have furniture for our friends when they arrive?" he asked, rolling a particularly large one away from the wall where he had knocked it aside.

"Of course," Shim agreed, glad she could do something to help. She took a deep breath and concentrated on calling the rocks back up from the ocean floor where they had rolled. She was very good at the levitation spells her mother had taught her. She used them for flying, and they also made cleaning up much easier. Soon the council hall looked as it had before Firzon began his angry pacing.

✦

Five days later, the dragons began to arrive. Fire-dragons crouched near the flaming lava flows in the back of the hall. Earth-dragons draped themselves over the boulders, water-dragons bobbed in the waves just outside the cave, and above all of them floated the air-dragons. The cave was only half full, because so many dragons had disappeared in the last years.

Once all the dragons had arrived, Firzon climbed to the top of a gigantic stone platform. There were pictures of all different kinds of dragons carved into the stone. Written so long ago that the words were hard to read was this saying:

Live fully,
Laugh loudly,
Gather wisdom and jewels,
And remember to play,
Say the dragons of today.

"My friends," began Firzon, "we are in a time of great peril. Humans are forgetting us. They do not see us when we fly in the sky, walk on the earth, swim in the water, or breathe fire over their heads. Many have tried to talk with them, but the humans on the boats called us 'whales,' and the people in the villages think we're clouds. They're even mining our treasures of gold and diamonds hidden in the earth. If we can't find a way to live in harmony with the humans, soon there will be no dragons left on earth."

"No, that can't be!" "A world without dragons!" "What will we do?" the dragons chorused, looking miserable and forlorn.

"There's still hope," Firzon shouted above the uproar of the other dragons. "We must put all of our magic into one last attempt to get the humans to see us and listen to us. No single dragon has enough magic to get the humans to notice us. But if all of us concentrate and let our magic flow into one dragon, that dragon might be able to stay in contact with the humans long enough to convince them to believe in magic again."

"That's a good idea," said Flimmer, an air-dragon with silver-blue scales.

"Who should go?" asked Sirserpent. He was looking bluer and healthier now that he was around all his friends, who were talking to him and touching him.

Firzon rose up to his full height, his pointed ears brushing the top of the high ceiling. "It must be a dragon everyone knows, so that you'll know exactly where to channel your magic. So I will go. Of all the dragons, I'm the oldest and best known of us all. I will go speak to these humans."

"No! Not you," protested Sirserpent, smacking the water with his wings and splashing some of it into the cavern. "Who will guide us if this plan doesn't work? Let *me* go. With more magic, I'm sure I will succeed this time. If I get larger and my neck grows longer, no human will ever call me a whale again!"

"It was a magnificent attempt that you and the other sea-dragons made." Firzon bowed his head toward Sirserpent. "But you are still weak, and the air-dragons don't know you as well as they know me."

Other dragons offered, but none of them were as well-known as Firzon. Then Shimilis spoke up from the back of the cavern. "Let me go," she said. All the dragons were silent as she strode through the hall and stepped onto the platform next to her father. "You all know me. I've met every one of you when you've come here to talk with my father."

"Out of the question. No. Absolutely not," stated Firzon. "You've never been out in the world among the humans. I've kept you here, protected from all that. I will be the one to go."

"But Sirserpent is right, Father. You must remain here in case we need to find another world. Only you, of all the dragons, have the knowledge and ability to move between worlds. With all of your magic pouring through me, I'll make sure to keep enough energy to fly home, no matter what happens when I meet the humans."

They talked and argued for hours until Shim finally got tired of it all and blew a bright-red flame straight across the cavern, right over the heads of the earth-dragons. "Listen to me," she said. "It's my right to make this quest."

"Your *right*?" challenged Firzon.

"Yes! Have you forgotten that I'm now one-thousand years old? Now that I've come of age, it's time for me to choose a quest –and I choose this one."

Firzon looked at her with surprise. "But, but... I thought that you'd decide to fly to the highest volcano on earth, or visit the craters on Venus or Mars. This is much too dangerous a journey for you."

"No, Shim is right," Flimmer said, gliding over their heads like a silver cloud. "It is her thousandth-birthday right to choose her own quest. And we all know her, just like we all know you. With you helping send magic to her, she'll be safe."

It took a few more hours of talking but they finally all agreed, including Firzon, though he wasn't happy about his daughter making this journey. Now they had to decide among all the human towns which village she would try to contact. The earth-dragons were most familiar with the humans, so they dragged out their stone books and looked into their crystals to search for a place.

Rocklinis gazed into a massive emerald crystal so intently that she began pushing it across the cave floor with her stubby nose. "Here it is! Here it is!" she cried. "I found the perfect place. It's even called 'Magik.' I'm sure the humans there must believe in magic."

"Yes, perfect!" agreed the other dragons.

"But if they believe in magic, why did they misspell it?" asked Shimilis, sounding doubtful.

"Maybe they forgot how to spell the word when they forgot that magic was real," Rocklinis suggested, turning and giving Shim a very toothy grin. "I'm sure they must believe in it now, because these records say that they changed the town's name to 'Magik' very recently. So when you remind them that dragons are real, you can also correct the name of the town and change the 'K' to a 'C'."

For the next five days all the dragons practiced sending Shim their magical energy. First she used it to grow as large as her father. She also worked hard on making her wings the most beautiful of rainbow colors, and her scales began to shine like the sun. Everyone agreed she was the most magnificent-looking dragon they had ever seen. The humans would have to acknowledge that dragons were real now!

Her father made Shim practice judging the amount of magical energy she had over and over again, so that she'd have enough left to fly home if she had problems talking with the humans. "The last thing you must practice is mind to mind speech at a distance. Find Flimmer and talk to him," Firzon said.

Shimilis concentrated hard, searching for Flimmer, who was flying beyond the sea near the land of the humans. Once she felt a tinge of his silver-blue essence she focused on forming her words clearly. *:Flimmer? Is that you? Can you hear me?:*

:That's good. But you're coming through a bit fuzzy. Don't work so hard at it. Just think in your mind as though you are talking to me in your head:

Shim relaxed and trusted the words to travel magically to him. *:How's this? I'm imagining telling you that the humans are seeing me and being friendly:*

:That's perfect. I can hear you clearly:

Finally she was ready to begin her journey to Magik. All the dragons took their places in the great council hall. Firzon climbed up on the platform and brought out his largest crystal. Shimilis felt the energy pouring into her from her father and all their friends.

"I'll find a way for us to live on this earth with the humans," she promised as she sprang into the morning air.

She flew quickly over the mountains, across the ocean, and over the land crowded with human towns. The earth-dragons sent her encouragement and the directions to find Magik. She finally saw it nestled against some hills, with farmlands on one side.

She spotted some humans working in the fields so she landed nearby, careful not to crush their new plants. Pulling all the magic she could from her dragon kin, she carefully approached the humans.

"Hello!" Shim said loudly.

"Did you say something, Ted?" one of the men asked his friend who was working a few rows away.

"Not me," Ted replied. "I didn't hear anything."

"*I* said 'Hello,'" the dragon told them. "I've come to ask why you no longer believe in magic. And why won't you talk to dragons anymore?"

"There it goes again," complained the first man. "Are you sure you aren't playing tricks on me, Ted?"

"It wasn't me, Juan. But I did hear some crows cawing in the distance. Maybe that's what you're hearing," Ted replied.

"I'm not a crow!" Shimilis insisted, rising to her full height and flapping her enormous wings. "I'm a fire-dragon, and I'm trying to talk to you."

"Feels like the wind's coming up," Juan said. "We'd better finish up in case there's a storm brewing."

Shimilis was so frustrated that she decided to blow a stream of fire over their heads to get their attention, just as she had done at the council meeting. She filled her lungs with air, ignited the fire in the back of her throat, and prepared to blow a mighty blast of flame. "Aghhh," she exhaled. But only a faint light came from her mouth along with a warm puff of air.

"I think it's warming up again," Juan remarked. "And it's getting a bit brighter, too. Maybe that storm isn't coming after all."

"No, no, you must see me," Shimilis wailed.

:Careful, daughter: Shim heard her father's voice in her head. :Do not despair, or you will lose magic even faster. Try finding another group of humans to approach, and we'll send you more magic:

Shimilis walked away from the two humans and immediately began feeling better. She sprang up into the air and flew over the town, searching for humans who might see and talk with her. Filled with magic, she was as large as her father, and the shadows from her rainbow-colored wings covered half the town. The humans looked up and started calling to one another, "Look at those gigantic clouds. There must be a terrible storm coming."

"No," Shimilis shouted in a loud voice, "it isn't a storm. It's me flying overhead. I'm a dragon, and I've come to Magik to bring you greetings from all the dragons."

"Listen to that thunder," yelled the people. "It must be a huge storm. We'd better go inside."

"Don't leave!" cried Shimilis. "Look, can a storm-cloud blow fire?" and she sent a streak of fire over the town, careful to make sure she didn't burn anything.

"Oh no, lightning!" screamed the humans. "It's so close. Run! Run!" All the humans scurried into their houses, slammed the doors, and closed all the shutters on their windows.

Shim landed in the empty square in the center of town. She wasn't feeling very good. She had an upset stomach, a headache, and she felt very weak. Focusing her thoughts carefully, she sent a message to Firzon. *:Father, you were right! Being ignored is the most terrible feeling!:*

:Come back now, while you still can: he told her.

:I'll try for a little longer: Shimilis responded. Then she straightened her wings and told herself, "I *will* find a way. I know I can." She looked around the place she'd landed. In the center of the town square there was a statue of a man wearing a suit and a tall hat. He had a scowl on his face. Underneath the statue were the words:

Frederick T. Magik,
Founder of the Magik Banking Corporation
Work hard,
Be productive and serious,
And riches will be yours.

Just looking at the statue and reading its message made Shimilis shrink down to the size of a human house. Her wings lost their sparkle. "Oh my, oh dear," she said to herself, since no one else would listen to her. "Maybe we picked the wrong town. I should fly back and let them know we'll not find help in this place." So Shimilis spread her wings, crouched down as low as she could, and with all her strength sprang up into the air. Instead of soaring high above the town of Magik, though, she wobbled in the air, nearly hitting the tops of two buildings. She narrowly missed a tall tree, then came crashing down in a park a short distance from the town square.

Shimilis slumped on the ground and rested her head on her forelegs. Tiny little flames began to appear all over her body as bits of her disappeared, until she was smaller than the tree she lay next to.

:*Father:* she cried. :*I'm afraid I'll melt into fire, just like the other dragons turned into air, water, or earth. I don't feel so solid anymore:*

:*Hang on:* he said, sending her as much magic as he could. :*Rest. Stay away from the humans and we will send you the strength to return home. Then we'll all leave the earth and find a new place where we are seen and respected by other beings:*

Shimilis slept in the park for many hours, dreaming of her mountain home and all her friends there. She was woken by something that she didn't recognize. It was the most wonderful, incredible sound. She rose up so she could hear it better and see where the noise was coming from. It was the sound of laughter. There were many small humans running around in a nearby meadow. There was a young boy wearing a blindfold who was weaving about shouting and laughing. All the other children were running around him, giggling and calling out his name.

The laughter sounded inviting and gave her hope, so Shim decided to try talking with the smaller humans. She moved quietly through the trees behind them, her best rainbow scales glowing. She drifted toward them feeling more like a cloud of colors than a dragon. Her faint wings were glistening, making it look as though jewels were hanging in the air.

When she approached them, all the children pointed at her, exclaiming with joy at the sparkles and flashes of red, purple, silver, and gold. They crowded around, touching and stroking her wings.

"Hey, where'd you all go?" cried the boy wearing the blindfold.

"Thomas, come over here and see what we found," called a little girl who was busy climbing up Shim's back.

Thomas took off the scarf and ran over to where the children were playing. "Who are you?" he asked the dragon.

"I'm a fire-dragon. My name is Shimilis, but you can call me Shim. I came here to talk with humans."

"I'm a human," stated Thomas. "Do you want to talk with me?"

"Oh, yes!" exclaimed Shimilis. "I've been trying to find humans who could see me."

"I see you!" said Thomas. "Can I crawl on your neck?" Shimilis lowered her head and Thomas climbed up. Shim felt wonderful. She was being seen again! She could feel herself become stronger and heavier as all the children cried out excitedly at her jeweled eyes, her silver claws, and her shimmering scales. They laughed as they swung from Shim's tail and played with her wings.

When the sun was straight overhead, some grown-up humans came out to the park. "It was nice that the storm didn't bring any rain so we can still have our picnic," they said to each other. They brought out tablecloths and dishes of food and placed them on the picnic tables. After a little while, they called the children over to join them.

"Come on," Thomas said to Shimilis. "We'll show you to our parents."

"Yeah, won't they be surprised to see what we found in the park today?" agreed the other children.

The dragon came along with them, and the children happily introduced their new friend to their parents. "Look who we met under the trees! Her name is Shimilis," they said. "Isn't she beautiful?" "Can she eat lunch with us?"

"What are you talking about?" asked the adults. "It's time to eat. Hurry up, the food's all ready."

"Can't you see our new friend?" chorused all the children.

"She's a fire-dragon," explained Thomas. "She's magical!"

"Oh, magic. Of course we see her," said a few of the parents, while looking in the wrong direction. "Now come on, it's time for lunch. What do you want to drink?"

"No, the dragon is right here, not over there!" yelled the children.

Several of the parents put their hands on their hips and frowned. "That's enough of playing games now." "Don't tell lies." "There's no such thing as a dragon."

As the adults stared right through her, Shim started feeling itchy all over and her stomach began to hurt.

"Why can't the grown-ups see you?" asked one little girl. Shimilis didn't know what to say. She could tell that it was very strange for the children to have their parents say she didn't exist. Especially since they had just been crawling all over her and knew the velvety feel of her wings, the warmth of her breath, and the slipperiness of her scales.

A tall girl with long braids gave Shim a sad smile, then turned her back on the dragon and said to the adults, "Yes, we were just playing. Some of the younger kids wanted to imagine a dragon, so we went along with them."

"Wasn't that a fun make-believe game?" an older boy added, walking away from Shim toward the tables filled with food. One by one, each child agreed that *not* seeing dragons was a very grown-up thing to do. "Pretending to see magical dragons is fun. Let's do it again tomorrow," said a little girl, looking right through Shimilis as though she wasn't there. In the end, Thomas was the only one who still insisted that he saw the dragon.

"I *do* see her. I do!" he shouted, holding onto the end of the dragon's wing. He kept refusing to say that his new friend wasn't real, so he was sent off to a corner of the meadow until he could come back and apologize to the grown-ups for being so rude.

"They're the ones being rude," Thomas told Shimilis, who followed him across the meadow. He sat down on the grass and the dragon lay down next to him. Her head hung down low. Tears started rolling from her eyes, but they would vanish by the time they reached the end of her long nose. She could feel herself starting to disappear. She was only able to receive the tiniest thread of energy coming from her father and the other dragons now. She had lost so much of her magic that she knew she would not have enough energy to fly back home and join her family and friends. All that was keeping her in this world was Thomas.

"I'm sorry that no one can see you, Shimmy. I think you're beautiful. I'd take you home with me, but you're too big," said Thomas.

Too big? Shim thought to herself. *Maybe I* am *too big. Is that why people don't see me? They just can't believe in something so big and so magical. Maybe it would help if I was smaller.* Flames danced along her back and down her tail as she thought about it. Using all her remaining magic, she began to shrink herself. Bit by bit, she got smaller and smaller. Her tail got very thin, but she could still curl it like a regular dragon's tail. Her body shrank quickly and became very tiny and thin. She had trouble getting her wings smaller. She concentrated very hard and they finally shrank, but they ended up sticking straight out from her body. Her head grew smaller but her eyes stayed large, like many-faceted crystals, so that she could still see the world through dragon eyes. Once she was little, she went zipping around the picnic tables, flying close to all the humans.

"Oh, look," they cried. "How pretty! The colors are so bright, and the wings beat so fast. We've never seen anything like it before!"

It worked! The humans could see her now. They all exclaimed over this new insect with the brilliantly colored body and odd wings. "It's some kind of new fly," said one man. Thomas ran forward and Shimilis landed on his hand. He proudly raised it up for all to see and said, "It's a dragonfly!"

The others tried to hold it, but the new dragonfly would only sit on Thomas's hand. His parents forgot that he was supposed to be off by himself, and they let him sit at the main table so everyone could admire the pretty creature. All the grown-ups came by to marvel at the beautiful dragonfly with wings that shone like the sun. Shimilis filled up with energy and love and started sending it back to the other dragons.

Now she had plenty of energy to talk with Firzon. *:Father:* she said, *:I've found a way for dragons to be seen and loved on the earth again. But I'm in a strange new form. I'm not sure what the other dragons will think of it:* Shim felt her father sensing her new form. She showed him her lacy, straight wings and her thin tail. But most of all, she could feel his surprise as he realized how small she was now.

:Let me talk with them: said Firzon. After a few minutes she heard his reply. *:They're all delighted to have a way to be seen again. The water-dragons have decided to be blue dragonflies, and the earth-dragons can be green. We fire-dragons will be red, and the air-dragons can be rainbow-colored. When we are alone or with other dragons, we can become our full selves again, but when we are around humans we will appear as dragonflies. Well done, daughter:* he added, and Shimilis could hear the pride and relief in his voice. *:This will also let us be around humans so we can find out what's happening in the world. Yes, this is a very good thing you have done. Enjoy your new friends, then come back so we can celebrate together:*

Shimilis flew around the humans, zipping over their heads and enjoying their praise. "Look at those wings! How fast they move." "Such a brilliant red color. I've never seen a brighter red."

Once everyone had gotten their food and started eating, the new dragonfly came back to Thomas and landed on his hand. He held Shimilis close and whispered to her, "I'm sorry you had to get so small for everyone to see you. But I'll always remember how big and beautiful you really are."

Shimilis whirled her wings and sang back to him, "It isn't how I look that matters to me. It's being seen and loved that's important. Being magical, I can be any size I want and I know it's still me inside, no matter what I look like on the outside. And when I find people like you, I can change my shape back to my big, beautiful self." She blew a tiny wisp of flame out her mouth to reassure him that she was still a real fire-dragon. Then she flew up and looked him in the eye with love. "Because of you, Thomas, and your belief in me, dragons and humans can now live happily together again."

The Hungry Ghost

✦

A long, long time ago, before humans lived on the earth, all the animals came together for a gigantic gathering. They loved the earth they walked on and the sky they lived under, but they were curious and full of questions. Why were they here on this planet? Was there something special they were supposed to do? They had a funny, slightly uncomfortable feeling that they were forgetting something very important, but they didn't know what it was. So they decided to gather together in a meadow so huge there was room for all the animals in the world. The giraffes came, the deer, the rhinoceros, and the panda bears. All kinds of cats wandered in, followed by jumping kangaroos. Mice and snakes crawled in, while owls and all the birds flew over them into the giant circle. A curious coyote paced back and forth under the trees at the edge of the meadow, watching everyone arrive. On the other side of the meadow ran a river that emptied into the sea. Not only were all the fuzzy, furred, and feathered creatures of the earth present at the meeting, but there was room for all the wet, watery, and scaly beings to also join together.

Once they had all arrived, they sent their voices up in a massive cry to the Creator of all life – who they called the Great Spirit – to ask why they were here on this earth. There was a tremendous clamor of brays, clucks, barking, and hooting. The noise drifted away across the plains and echoed against the mountains, calling out the questions: "Why? Why this world? Why us? Why are we here?" Then they were all silent, waiting.

Into the stillness the Great Spirit came. Each creature could hear in his or her own language the Great Spirit saying to them: "I heard your cry carried by the tallest trees and whispered on every wind. I will help each of you understand why you are here on this earth. The reason is too beautiful and wondrous to explain in mere words." Then they all felt the Great Spirit looking directly at each of them with deep love and caring, as it said, "You are very special. To accept and learn about that specialness, you must perform a task."

Magical bags appeared beside each of them. The bags were in all the colors of the earth: browns, blues, greens, pinks, and purples. They were made of a soft velvety material and could shrink into a tiny ball that could fit in a paw, hoof, or flipper, or be opened up large enough for the individual animal to crawl halfway inside. They were so strong that when the wolf stuck his head and front legs inside his bag, his claws did not tear the sides. And the elephants' tusks didn't harm their sacks either. Each bag was exactly the right size for each animal, bird, or fish to easily carry with them.

"Your task is to be aware and to pay careful attention to this world," the Great Spirit continued saying to each of them. "You will see wondrous sights, and sometimes you will find great mounds of marvelous food, jewels, and other beautiful objects, more bountiful than you have ever seen before. I have placed these treasure piles on this world just for you, and you may each take gifts from them to carry in your bag. When your sack is full, then you will have an understanding of why you are here."

All the creatures sat quietly and wondered about the words of the Great Spirit – except Coyote, who had stayed on the very edge of the meadow. As soon as he heard the words of the Great Spirit, Coyote jumped up, grabbed his sack, and ran off into the woods. As he slipped away from the other creatures, Coyote told himself, "I'm going to be the first one to fill up my sack. Everyone will be so impressed when I come back with my sack completely full. I'll have more than everyone else. I'll win!"

Because Coyote went dashing off to get ahead of the other animals, he didn't hear the end of the Great Spirit's speech. "The special mounds of treasures will only appear at certain times. They will not last long. Even as you are still admiring them, they will start to vanish. Do not worry if you cannot figure it out at the beginning. As your sack slowly fills up, you will begin to understand more and more." After uttering these words, the Great Spirit sent a final message of love to all the animals and then disappeared, leaving the animals alone to talk about what they had heard.

While the other animals were looking at their multicolored sacks, still puzzling over the Great Spirit's words, Coyote was running through the woods as fast as he could. He spun around a corner and there, between two small willow trees, the sun sparkled on a pile of pretty jewels, crystals, and gold. Not only were there beautiful treasures, there were plenty of good things to eat. There were also many gifts that were neither food nor jewels, but Coyote didn't stop to wonder what those things were. He was busy scooping as much as he could into his sack as fast as he could. "I can fill my whole sack from just this one pile!" he bragged to himself. "All the other animals will admire me and think I'm the best when they see me come back with it already filled up."

As he daydreamed about all the praise he would receive, he didn't notice that he was no longer alone in the woods. A hungry ghost had seen Coyote near the pile and had crept closer to find out what Coyote was doing. Hungry ghosts have tiny eyes and huge mouths. Their bodies are one big stomach, which looks like a gray, filmy shadow billowing behind their heads. Having such enormous mouths and stomachs they are always hungry, but they never fill up. They eat everything: food and feelings, things and thoughts. Like all ghosts, they are hard to see, and hungry ghosts are the hardest of all to spot because they like to sneak in and steal from other creatures. They have no hands, so the only way they can eat is if they can trick someone into throwing things into their large mouths.

The hungry ghost saw a great chance for a meal with Coyote, so it chewed through the end of his sack and put its mouth right where the bottom of the sack used to be. Coyote didn't notice anything because he was so busy shoveling all the bounty into the sack, and planning how he would show off his success to the others. Then something began to happen to all the beautiful objects in front of him.

"Stop!" Coyote yelled at the pile. "Don't disappear! I haven't taken all of you yet." He began to work faster and faster. Since he hadn't heard the end of the Great Spirit's message, he didn't realize that the mounds would naturally appear and disappear throughout the forest.

As the last of the pile vanished, Coyote said smugly to himself, "Well, it doesn't matter. I've just about filled up my sack. It'll be enough for me to be the winner of all the animals!" He looked inside to check how full his sack was, but instead of seeing it full of jewels and treasures, all he saw was the grey emptiness of the hungry ghost's stomach. The hungry ghost had devoured everything Coyote had thrown in its mouth. Since Coyote was no longer feeding it, the hungry ghost drifted off, leaving a ragged tear at the bottom of Coyote's empty bag. Coyote felt very angry and miserable because the hungry ghost had eaten Coyote's feelings of happiness, too. "What's wrong with my sack?" wailed Coyote. "The Great Spirit must have given me a damaged one." He hurriedly searched for some water reeds to weave together to repair the bottom of his bag. "I'll find another pile and *still* get the most!" he cried as he finished stitching up his sack. Then he ran off so fast he almost bumped into Bear, who was wandering through the forest.

"What's the hurry, Coyote?" called Bear. But Coyote was already ten trees away with his sack trailing behind him and a hungry ghost flying over his head. "Oh, Coyote always seems to be in such a hurry," Bear remarked to herself. As she looked about her, she noticed that the sun was shining into a small clearing in the woods. *This looks like a good place for a rest,* she thought, choosing a comfortable-looking tree and getting a good backrub from its knobby bark as she slid down it.

While she was resting, she noticed a glow off to one side through the trees. Curious, she lumbered over to see what it was. Heaped against the base of a huge tree was a mound of good food and flashing jewels, just like the Great Spirit had said would appear. *This is magnificent!* Bear thought. *I couldn't imagine anything this wonderful when the Great Spirit was talking. This whole pile could fill up my entire sack.* She swung her massive head from side to side, gazing at the assortment of riches. *But I don't think that's what the Great Spirit meant for us to do.* So Bear sat down near the pile to admire it, amazed by how large it was. Even though she had heard the Great Spirit say that the gifts would soon disappear, she carefully and slowly looked at each fascinating, glorious thing. When she noticed one especially lovely piece of honeycomb she smiled and wrinkled her nose, enjoying the inviting scent. *The honey is such a sweet golden shade and it looks so inviting, I think I'll take this one piece.*

As she was reaching for the honeycomb, a hungry ghost floated by. But when it saw how lovingly and carefully Bear was placing her treasure into her sack, it knew that it wouldn't be able to trick her and eat through the bottom of her bag. Once the honeycomb was lying in the sack, the ghost had no hands to reach in and steal it, so it flew off to try to find an animal more like Coyote. By the time Bear had arranged the honeycomb at the bottom of her sack and carefully licked each claw thoroughly, the rest of the pile had vanished. So Bear got up and decided to continue her walk through the forest.

✦

As the years passed, Bear's sack began to slowly fill up. She added to that first piece of honeycomb a brilliant yellow jewel that reminded her of the sun, and an opal to remind her of the moon. Then there was a pretty rock that hadn't been part of a special pile at all, but had glistened at her while she drank from a cool stream. There was a small stick from the first tree her cubs had climbed, and bark from the white willow tree she could chew on when she was feeling ill. All of these things and many more Bear lovingly carried in her sack.

Early on the hungry ghosts tried to get Bear to feed them. They whispered things like, "Hurry up. You don't have enough. You're not good enough. Everyone else has more. They're better than you."

But Bear would look in her sack and reply, "I have many treasures here. I have just the right amount for me." Then the hungry ghosts would get discouraged and leave her alone for many seasons.

Then one day she stumbled upon one of the Great Spirit's treasure hoards at the same time that Badger crawled around a bush and also spotted it. They both liked hazelnuts, and this pile was filled with them. Bear tried to grab as many as she could before Badger ate them all. She was so intent on stuffing the nuts into her sack that she didn't notice that a hungry ghost had opened its wide mouth over the top of her bag, and she was now throwing all the tasty nuts right into its cavernous stomach. Badger also had a ghost attached to the mouth of his bag. When he and Bear noticed that they had *both* been feeding the hungry ghosts, they sat down and laughed together.

"Well, here's the last hazelnut," Bear said, picking up a nut that had rolled under her bag. She gave it to Badger.

"Thank you. And here's one for you that I missed," remarked Badger, plopping a nut into Bear's mouth.

"Here are two more I missed!" exclaimed Bear, tossing them into Badger's open mouth.

"Wait! Here is a whole bunch of them hidden beneath this gold," announced Badger in a surprised voice. They continued discovering more and more nuts and feeding each other and the hungry ghosts hovered over them, waiting.

"I can't eat another one," Bear finally admitted after Badger fed her a really plump nut.

"I've never seen one of the Great Spirit's magnificent mounds stay around so long before," remarked Badger.

"I haven't really been hunting for the special piles of treats anymore," admitted Bear. "So I don't know how long they usually stay around."

"Then how did you get so many nice treasures in your sack?" asked Badger.

"I seem to find them all over. You probably wouldn't consider some of the things very special," Bear said, pulling a moss-covered rock out of her bag. "This reminds me of one of the best naps I ever had. All I have to do is put it by my head at bedtime, and the smell and the soft fuzzy moss make me feel so good that I have the most wonderful dreams while I sleep."

"Well, you don't have to worry about hungry ghosts trying to steal *that*. I've gotten so tired of having to watch out for them. They seem to cluster around the piles." Badger shooed one away that was flying low over the hoard in front of them. "I don't understand why the pile is still here. They usually disappear as soon as I start taking things from them."

"Here," said Bear, handing Badger a paw-full of nuts that she noticed toward the bottom of the pile. "Put these in your sack and don't let the hungry ghost near it." Then she saw a few blackberries. "Here are some berries to go with it, and a couple of pretty stones and jewels you might like." Bear continued giving Badger good things to eat and other riches for his collection, while Badger waved off the ghosts that flew around their heads."Can't you see we're not going to feed you?" he called to the ghosts. They stopped flying around and actually closed their mouths in surprise.

"Ha-ha!" laughed Bear. "They think they're so invisible, but we see them now and they aren't going to trick us again." The hungry ghosts quivered above them for a moment, then they rushed away as though they were scared of the two friends. With no bothersome ghosts around, they enjoyed filling Badger's sack, then they started finding fun things to place in Bear's bag. Just as they finished filling both sacks, the pile disappeared.

"Well, look at that. We stuffed our sacks completely full," stated Badger. "We've filled them up with friendship, good memories, and pieces of the world around us. Do you think that's what the Great Spirit wanted us to learn?"

"Maybe," Bear said thoughtfully.

Just then a very thin and tired-looking Coyote wandered into the clearing. "Are there any of those wonderful hoards of food around here?" he asked them hopefully. "The piles don't like me; they disappear as soon as I start grabbing from them."

"You just missed one, but I do have some food to share with you," said Bear. Both she and Badger gave him some of their nuts and berries, and Bear even had some honey to offer him. When he was feeling better, Coyote went off to continue his search. Bear turned to Badger and said, "Well, now our sacks are no longer completely full. Though for all that Coyote ate, it didn't seem to shrink my treasure too much."

"I'm actually glad mine isn't filled up completely anymore. I don't know what I'd do if I wasn't roaming the forest looking for things to put in my collection."

"Well, Coyote ate enough that we don't have to worry about that anymore. We can still search for more. Shall we do it together?" suggested Bear.

"Yes, let's journey together!" agreed Badger. And the two creatures ambled off in search of more treasures. To this day, Bear and Badger can often be seen wandering leisurely through the woods together, or sharing treats from their sacks with other animals. But Coyote is most often glimpsed running through the woods, still frantically hunting for more and more mounds of treasures to stuff into his sack – and the hungry ghosts like to follow him wherever he goes.

Cat's Gift

✦

As soon as Rosa got home from school, she ran up the stairs to her room as fast as she could. She didn't stop for the treats on the kitchen table or remember to take her boots off at the front door. It was her eighth birthday, and there on her bed lay the beautiful jeweled box.

"Do I have to wait until after dinner?" Rosa asked her mother, who had followed her into her room.

"Yes, and you need to get those shoes off before you track more dirt all over the house."

"Tell me about the gift again," begged Rosa as she sat on her bed tugging at her red boots.

"You know the story so well you could tell it to me," her mother said laughing. "Well, this is the gift your father received when he was eight years old. And your grandmother was eight when she was given it. And your great-grandmother was...."

"Eight!" filled in Rosa.

"... when her father presented it to her. The gift goes so far back that no one remembers where it first came from, or who made it. In each generation of your father's family, this gift is given to the eldest child on their eighth birthday. They can use it and play with it as long as they want. Then they save it for their first child, just as your father kept it downstairs on the mantel over the fireplace, waiting for you."

Rosa stroked the jeweled box. "Can I take a little peek? I'm eight now."

"No, your father and grandmother would never forgive me if I let you open it before they got here."

Rosa waited at the living room window until she saw her father's car crawling along the street toward their house. She danced next to the driveway as they drove up, then skipped around to the passenger door and opened it for her grandmother. "Grandma, Grandma! You came!" Rosa sang to her.

"Of course I did. Your father picked me up on his way home. I'd never miss your eighth birthday." Her eyes shone extra brightly as she looked down at her granddaughter.

Rosa grabbed them both by the hand and pulled them inside. Her mother had come home early from work, so dinner was already prepared. It was a broccoli and bean casserole, Rosa's favorite, but she only picked at it as she waited for everyone else to finish eating. When her mom handed her a piece of cake, Rosa put it to the side. "I'll eat it later. Can I open my presents now?"

"Yes," her father said. "And I know which one you want first." He picked up the jeweled box and carefully placed it on Rosa's lap.

Rosa slowly ran her fingers around the edge, feeling the bumps and curves. "Oh, it tickles!" Holding her breath and scrunching her lips together firmly, she raised the lid. The smell of cedar and dry leaves drifted up from the box. The first thing she saw was a layer of purple velvet. It felt smooth and creamy as Rosa moved it aside, uncovering an intricately carved wooden cat. Every detail was so precisely carved that for a moment Rosa thought the cat was real. It was striped with the grain of the wood, flowing from dark brown to creamy gold. The eyes were two emeralds, a rich deep green. Whiskers were painted on, beginning at the red jeweled nose and running along both sides of the head. Around the cat's neck was a shimmering necklace with a large, flat amber stone that had the word "Amarisa" carved on it. The cat was sitting upright with its tail wrapped around its front paws, so that it stood firm and tall upon the table where Rosa placed it.

They stared at each other unblinking until her grandmother said, "Touch it. Pet it like you would pet my cat Dover."

Rosa reached out her hand and ran it down the smooth wood on Amarisa's back. The wood had been stroked for so many generations that Rosa's hand glided over a surface as soft as fur. "She's beautiful." Remembering her manners, Rosa ran over to her father. "Thank you, Daddy," she whispered, wrapping her arms around him.

In between opening her other presents, she petted Amarisa. And when it was time to get ready for bed Rosa laid the cat beside her on her pillow. After she'd been tucked in, read a story, and left alone for the night, she turned to the cat and said, "Hello, Amarisa." A light glinted in the emerald-green depths of the cat's eyes. "You're so pretty. You look like a real cat." As she stroked the head, she noticed the whiskers were standing straight out from the face. "Oh, I thought those were painted on!" Then more loudly, she said "Oh!" when Amarisa opened her mouth to show a very pink tongue. A huge yawn enlarged the cat's face and her ears flattened against the top of her head. Then Amarisa shook herself and stretched, arching her back high and extending her legs far out in front. Her tail lashed back and forth as if it had been imprisoned too long.

"Hello, Rosa," Amarisa said, and then she yawned again.

"H-hello, Amarisa," stammered Rosa. "Who . . . who are you? How can you talk to me? And how do you know my name?"

"I heard your mother say it. I can always talk when people talk to me – and when I want to talk to them, of course. As for who I am. Well, I'm me of course. Who else would I be?" Amarisa said all this while wandering around the bed inspecting the pillow and sniffing at the teddy bear propped up against it.

Rosa didn't know how to respond, so she introduced Amarisa to all her stuffed animals and got a special quilted blanket down from the closet for her to sleep on. The next day Rosa took the cat to school for show-and-tell. "This is Amarisa," Rosa proudly proclaimed, holding up the wooden cat. "I was given her for my eighth birthday." Everyone thought the cat was very beautiful, but when Rosa said she was a talking cat everyone laughed. "No, really, she can speak!" Rosa cried out above the noise. "We were talking together last night about my stuffed animals."

"What did your stuffed animals say?" jeered a boy named Jeff from the back.

"Stuffed animals don't talk," replied Rosa, "but Amarisa does." She held the cat high above her head. Even though the perch was a bit shaky, Amarisa remained as wooden as she looked. She didn't move an inch to try to balance herself as Rosa's arm wobbled.

"That's very nice, Rosa," said the teacher, motioning for the class to quiet down. Then she turned to the girl sitting behind Rosa. "Sara, did you have something to share with us today?"

Rosa took her seat, carefully wrapping the cat in the purple velvet cloth and placing her in the jeweled box. She was disappointed that Amarisa hadn't said anything to the class, and a little afraid that her conversation with the cat the night before might have only been a dream. When Rosa got home from school she raced to her room and unloaded her backpack. On top was Amarisa's box. She opened the lid and waited. As soon as the cat crawled out, Rosa let out a big sigh. "You *are* alive! Why didn't you talk to the class? They think you're only wood and jewels."

Amarisa enjoyed a huge yawn before turning to Rosa. "I didn't hear any of them talking to me."

"Of course they didn't. They didn't know you're a real cat. And a talking one too!"

"If I have to prove that I'm real before they give me the courtesy of saying hello, then they will have to wait a long, long time for me to talk to them."

"I don't understand."

Amarisa reached a paw around to wash her ear. "I don't understand why they didn't talk to me either. Don't worry about them. Come over to the window and I'll tell you about the different trees you can see from here, and how trees affect the weather."

The next day Rosa tried talking to her mother about Amarisa, but her mother just thought it was cute that Rosa pretended Amarisa could talk. "Why don't you talk to your dad about the cat? He used to play with it when he was a boy," her mom suggested.

"Ok, I will," said Rosa. But her father was always so busy that it never seemed to be the right time to ask him. So instead of talking to others about Amarisa, she spent many nights talking with Amarisa herself.

"How come the sky is blue?" Rosa asked Amarisa, who told her about sunlight and colors. "Why do birds eat bugs?" Rosa asked, which led to a long discussion about the balance of life and death, and how the death of some species brings life to others.

"Why are people so mean?" Rosa demanded one night.

"Are all people mean?" asked Amarisa.

"No, not all, just at school. Jeff calls me 'show-off' and 'teacher's pet' because I know the answers so often."

"Are you showing off?"

"No," responded Rosa quickly. Amarisa just looked at her. "Well, maybe. It's really neat knowing the answers. The teacher used to call on Jeff the most. Now she calls on me! Last week I told them what you'd said about rain and thunder and lightning. The teacher thought I was so smart. I guess it isn't fair if everyone doesn't have a friend like you to talk to."

"Maybe if you let Jeff answer more questions, he'd be nicer to you."

"I'll try."

Whenever Rosa was not talking with Amarisa, she would carefully place the cat on top of the jeweled box on her dresser. There she would sit as though she was just a fancy plaything, until Rosa spoke to her. Over the years a few of Rosa's special friends would pet and greet the cat, and then Amarisa would begin talking with them. By the time Rosa had a sleepover for her twelfth birthday, she was able to invite five friends who all knew and treated Amarisa with respect.

After the presents were opened and the cake was eaten, Rosa and her friends went up to her bedroom. Sara, the first of her friends to talk with Amarisa, went right to the shelf where the cat was sitting and asked, "Can you tell me why my grandfather died? I miss him. I didn't want him to die. My mom cries all the time now, and so do I." Amarisa stretched and yawned, showing her pink tongue. All the girls waited. They'd met Sara's grandfather and were also sorry that he had died.

"What is life and death?" Amarisa asked them. None of the girls answered. "If you form a circle on the carpet, I will help each of you find your own unique answer." They all sat down on the floor and looked up at the cat in anticipation. Amarisa brought her front paw up and licked it, then rubbed her whole face with it, paying special attention to her whiskers. "There is life before life, and life after life," she said. "A birth is always a death. And death is always another birth. Lie down with your heads in the center of the circle and close your eyes. I'll try to show you something that might help you understand." She jumped down from the dresser and walked around the circle, touching each of them on the top of their heads with her nose.

"Oh, what's happening?" exclaimed Sara. "I'm floating on a cloud of rainbows!"

"You're seeing and experiencing different worlds, and you are seeing this world as other creatures see it," explained Amarisa. "I'm showing you this so you'll know that this world and this life are not the only options there are."

"I'm seeing a forest!" exclaimed Rosa. "Oh, this must be how a tree feels about falling down. Look at how the green shoots grow out of its trunk!"

A little while later, Ruth called out, "Wow, it's like at school when we looked at the pictures about the different religions."

"Which one?" asked Rosa.

"All of them."

After a while, Amarisa touched each of them again to bring them back to Rosa's room. As they sat up and looked around, Amarisa said to Sara, "You'll still miss your grandfather because he's no longer in a physical body – but now you know that there are other realities. Life always goes on, but not in the same form or in the same way."

When Sara returned home the next day her mother was in the kitchen crying. "Mom, are you sad about Grandpa?" Her mother nodded. "You should go talk with Rosa's cat. She showed us all these different worlds, and we could see so many varieties of life. It was amazing! The world felt smaller after Grandpa left, but now it feels big and wonderful again. I still miss him, and we can't play games anymore, but I feel better after talking with Amarisa. Maybe she could help you too."

While Sara was talking, her mother turned and stared at her daughter. "What are you talking about, Sara? What cat? Cats can't talk."

"This one can, Mom. Her name is Amarisa and she's Rosa's cat. I've talked with her lots of times, but she's never shown us anything like this before. She touched my forehead and suddenly I was seeing these strange worlds."

"What kind of a cat is it? Does Rosa's mother know about this? What kind of things does Rosa do with her black cat?"

"She's not black, Mom, she's all shades of brown. She's really pretty, with stripes and green eyes. And she's super-smart. She told us about life and death and about Grandpa and. . . ."

"I don't want to hear any more about this," her mother interrupted. "And I don't want you to have anything more to do with Rosa's cat, or Rosa either. We've told you what happened to your grandfather and where he is now." She got up and headed for the telephone. "I'm checking with the other parents. I want to find out how long this has been going on."

Sara's mother called the parents of all the other girls and told them what their daughters had been doing during the sleepover. She suggested they all meet to uncover the truth together.

After all the parents had arrived at Rosa's house, Sara's mother insisted on seeing the cat. Rosa was very scared having all these grownups wanting to know about Amarisa. She went back to her room and whispered to the cat, "You've got to talk to the parents of my friends and tell them the wonderful things you tell me. Otherwise they might be mad at me and punish me. And I didn't do anything wrong. Please, promise me you'll speak to them."

"It depends how they treat me," Amarisa said, as she focused on licking her paw. She kept her head down and didn't look at Rosa.

"Just this once, say something to them, even if they're rude to you. Please, for me."

"Maybe," was all Amarisa would agree to, and she walked over to her jeweled box and gracefully climbed in.

Rosa brought the box downstairs and opened it up to show the beautifully carved cat inside. She told all the adults, "This is the cat that talks to me. You have to be polite so she will talk to you too."

"Well, I never," said Sara's mother loudly, "Where does she get off telling us to be polite?"

"And to a wooden cat!" added Ruth's father.

The adults all agreed that Rosa was being rude, and they began talking loudly among themselves.

"Go ahead, say something," Rosa said to her cat friend.

Amarisa steadied herself on Rosa's hands, then she raised her whiskers and with exaggerated politeness said, "Excuse me," then again, "Excuse me." But the adults were making so much noise talking back and forth above Rosa's and Amarisa's heads that none of them heard the cat talk.

Rosa shouted, "Be quiet, you're not listening to her!"

"Rosa!" Her mother put a restraining hand on her daughter's shoulder. "I want you to apologize – now."

"No," cried Rosa, "it's not fair." Her mother began apologizing for her behavior and trying to calm the other parents. Rosa looked down at Amarisa perched in her hands. Her tail was swishing back and forth, but the adults weren't paying any attention. Rosa's mother was talking to the others, explaining how the cat was a traditional gift in her husband's family. Rosa wished that her father wasn't away on a business trip. He was the only adult who would nod and smile happily when she shared with him something Amarisa had said.

The cat looked around once more at the adults, then her whiskers drooped until they were flat against her head, making them look like they were painted on. She wrapped her tail around her paws and slowly became silent and still.

The adults finally grew quiet. "I'm sorry Rosa, dear," Sara's mother said, "You just turned twelve, so if you want to believe your toy cat can talk, I guess we shouldn't scold you." She glanced at Rosa's mother, who smiled encouraging. "Sara outgrew make-believe years ago. But if you want to, go ahead and have the cat talk to us."

Rosa turned quickly to Amarisa and said, "Okay, you can talk now. They'll be polite and listen." But the cat remained solid as stone. Rosa begged the cat to talk and move, but it did nothing.

"Oh, I heard the cat," said Sara's mother. "It said 'Happy Belated Birthday, Rosa.'" All the adults laughed.

"Does pretty kitty want some milk?" asked Ruth's father.

Rosa tucked Amarisa under her arm and ran crying up to her room.

"My, my," commented Sara's mother, "and I used to think she was so mature for her age. Well, let her know that Sara won't be able to come over next weekend. We have so much to do that she just won't have any time. I'm sure you understand." Then she and the other parents left.

Rosa's mother went up to her room to look for her. She found Rosa lying on her bed sobbing into her pillow. She looked around for the cat, but didn't see her anywhere. The jeweled box was on Rosa's desk. But it was closed tight, and a stack of books was piled on top of it.

"I'm sorry, Rosa," her mom told her. "I know you like to pretend that you talk with your cat, but now that you're twelve I think you're getting too old for those kinds of games." Rosa just cried harder. Her mother sat with her for a few minutes, then got up and said, "Go ahead and cry. I know you're sad. If you want to talk about it, I'll be in the den." But Rosa didn't want to talk to anyone about it. Later she begged her mom not to tell her dad anything about it when he got back from his business trip. Her father had given Amarisa to her, so she was afraid he'd be mad at her if he knew she'd gotten into trouble because of the cat.

After her twelfth birthday, when Rosa would ask Ruth, "Do you want to spend the night this weekend?"

Ruth would look down at her shoes and say, "I'm too busy." Or "My mom said I can't."

Sara and the rest of her friends would say the same kinds of things, and no one asked Rosa to play at their houses anymore. When Sara's younger brother heard about Rosa's cat and the sleepover, he started calling her "Ms. Make-believe" at school. Others started using the nickname too, and soon Rosa dreaded going to school. She didn't want to be known as the girl who pretended to talk to cats, so she stopped asking Amarisa questions in the evening. Then school got even worse, because she didn't know as many of the answers and her teacher quit calling on her in class.

One day Sara's brother and his friends followed her all the way home meowing at her. Rosa rushed into the house and ran straight to her room. She grabbed the jeweled box with Amarisa shut tightly inside and flung it into the back of her closet. "I never want to talk to you again," Rosa cried. "You didn't talk to the adults, and now see what's happened! I hate you!" Amarisa's box settled into the farthest dusty corner, and over time it was covered up by piles of old toys and dolls.

As Rosa grew older, she made new friends. She went to college and eventually got married and had a daughter of her own. Her parents brought over her old playthings, including the cat's jeweled box. By now, Rosa had convinced herself that the cat had been a cute imaginary friend she'd had as a child, and she was pleased to pass it on to her daughter, Claire. On Claire's eighth birthday, Rosa gave her the jeweled box with the cat inside.

Claire loved her new toy and played with it all evening. When it was time to go to sleep she took the cat to bed and laid it beside her on the pillow. As soon as she was alone, she began talking to the cat. As she spoke to it, the cat's eyes flashed and its whiskers stood up, and it spoke to Claire.

As Rosa was getting ready to go to bed, she decided to check on her daughter one more time. When she came to the door, she heard her daughter talking. She slowly opened the door a crack to investigate. Claire was propped up in bed facing away from her. At first Rosa thought she was talking to her teddy bear. When she saw the bear at the foot of the bed, she realized that her daughter was talking to the wooden cat. As she continued to watch from the doorway, she heard the cat talking back. Then the cat rose up off the pillow and stared at Rosa with the same bright green eyes she remembered as a child.

No, this can't be happening, Rosa thought to herself, *it's not real. Amarisa was only imaginary.* She gripped the door frame to steady herself. When Amarisa yawned and Rosa saw the cat's twitching whiskers and pink tongue, memories of many late-night talks overwhelmed her. *What should I do?* she wondered. *Should I leave and let Claire have her friend for as long as she can? But I don't want her to get hurt like I did. Maybe I should go in and put an end to it right now, before she starts to love Amarisa. I could shut the cat up in her box and hide her away from Claire. But could I do that to Amarisa? It wasn't her fault that I got teased as a kid.* The questions kept bouncing about in Rosa's mind as she stood at the door looking at Amarisa. The cat stared back at her, twitching her whiskers until Claire turned to see who the cat was gazing at.

"Mommy," she exclaimed, "come see! The cat can talk. Her name is Amarisa."

"Yes, I know she talks," said Rosa, coming slowing into the room. She sat on the bed and reached out a hand to pet Amarisa. "What am I going to do with you?" she asked the cat.

"Keep scratching my chin," replied Amarisa. Glancing first at Claire, then back at Rosa, she added, "Maybe with the two of you together, this time it will be different."

"But how can it be different?" Rosa asked. "Don't you remember how terrible it was for me?"

"What was so terrible, Mommy?" asked Claire. Amarisa stared at Rosa, waiting for her response.

"Actually, in the beginning it was wonderful. But one day Amarisa wouldn't talk to the parents of my friends. Then everyone teased me and my friends wouldn't play with me. I got so angry that I locked Amarisa in her box and never talked to her again."

"That would be bad," agreed Claire. "I wouldn't like it if my friends stopped playing with me."

Amarisa's head hung down, and she said softly, "I couldn't talk to them."

"I know, you didn't like speaking to people if they were rude to you," Rosa said stroking Amarisa's soft fur.

"The truth is," the cat said, staring down at her paws, "I *couldn't* talk. I just made it seem like I was choosing not to talk. But whenever too many people believe I'm not real, I go all wooden and solid and can't make a sound."

"You never told me that!" Rosa said.

"I was too ashamed. I thought you wouldn't like me as much if you knew I wasn't able to do everything you wanted me to."

"I might've been a little bit disappointed, but I would've loved you all the same. If I'd known, I wouldn't have been so mad and locked you away and never talked to you again. I thought you didn't love me enough to talk to my friends' parents."

"Oh, I loved you so much!" Amarisa purred and rubbed Rosa's hand. "I tried so hard to never let you down or disappoint you. I was embarrassed that I couldn't talk whenever I wanted to."

"What does M-bear-est mean, Mommy?" Claire asked.

"Embarrassed is that pain you have inside when you think something is wrong with you and you want to hide it so no one knows about it," explained Rosa. "It's also when you make a mistake and people laugh at you, or you're afraid they will laugh or tease you."

"Like when I wet the bed at Julia's and I tried to hide the sheets?" Claire asked.

"Yes. And embarrassment feels worse when you aren't able to talk about it. Remember how you felt better when Julia's mother found the sheets and told you Julia has accidents at night too?"

"Yeah. Then she let me put the soap in the washing machine and push the buttons to wash the sheets." Claire turned to Amarisa. "I'm sorry you felt bad inside. Maybe if you met some other cats who also can't talk when people don't believe in them, you'll feel better."

Amarisa licked Rosa's hand with her pink tongue, "Your daughter is right. And I'm sorry. I should've told you right away why I couldn't speak to the adults that day."

"That's ok, I'm just glad you're back." Rosa wiped away a tear with the sleeve of her shirt. "Now, with all three of us talking together, we can make it different this time."

"Don't you mean 'four of us'?" asked Claire.

"Four?" Rosa and Amarisa asked together.

"Yeah – Grandpa! When you gave me the box tonight, he said that he had the cat before you. So he can talk with us too."

"Oh!" exclaimed Rosa. She carefully picked up the jeweled box and began turning it over in her hands. More tears slowly flowed down her cheeks.

"What's wrong, Mommy?" asked Claire.

"I just realized that I never told my dad about what happened with Amarisa. I remember he asked a few times why I wasn't playing with her anymore, but I was afraid he'd be upset with me, and so I never said anything to him. He could've helped me, if only I'd let him know. But the truth is that I was too embarrassed to talk to him."

"I'd love to see him again."Amarisa climbed on top of the box and stood up tall. "My magic increases the more people talk to me. So with all four of us together, we can do wonderful things and have lots of fun together."

The next day Rosa, Claire, and Amarisa surprised Rosa's father with a visit. He was very glad to see all of them, especially the furry one who curled up in his lap. As Claire grew up, they all made sure that she never had to forsake her talking cat friend.

The Blind Bunny

✦

Once upon a time there was a young bunny named Timmer. One sparkling morning, when the air smelled of wet grass and ripe berries, Timmer was hopping around in the meadow in front of his home. His mother came out of the family burrow and waved him over. "Do you remember meeting your cousin Karin last summer?" she asked.

Timmer bounced up and down, his ears waving wildly. "Oh, yes! She was really fun to play with."

"Karin, her parents, and all her brothers and sisters are moving to our meadow. They'll be our neighbors. Since Karin is blind, I want you to make a special effort to help her get adjusted. Will you promise to show her around and make sure she feels at home here?"

"Yes, Mom, I'd be happy to. I'll do a good job, you'll see."

When Karin and her family arrived, Timmer showed his blind cousin all the best places to eat: where the sweetest grass grew, and where the most tender leaves could be found. He even took her to his favorite bush and let her snuggle underneath it where the earth was especially soft. He made sure she knew all the paths and tunnels so she wouldn't get lost.

Timmer enjoyed being with Karin and looking out for her. One day he noticed that she wasn't with all the rest of the bunnies, who were over in the meadow that had a stream running right down the middle of it. He quickly went hopping around looking for her. She wasn't in any of the tunnels or by his favorite bush. She wasn't even by the new patch of tender lettuce he'd shown her yesterday. He finally found her all by herself in the meadow where the weeping willows hung low. She looked so alone with no other bunnies around her that he ran down to her as quickly as he could.

"Karin!" he called as he bounded up to her. "Here you are. I was looking all over for you."

"Hi, Timmer," Karin replied.

"I'm sorry that you got separated from the other bunnies and ended up over here all by yourself. You must be so lonely."

"Lonely? But I'm not alone."

"Yes, you are. You're here by yourself. All the other bunnies are in the meadow with the stream."

"But I could hear a bunny whistling happily right over there." She twitched her ears toward the edge of the meadow. "I wasn't alone."

"Whistling?" Timmer asked, wondering if there was something wrong with her ears as well as her eyes. Then he listened, and he did hear a sound like a bunny whistling. He lifted one long ear into the air so he could hear better. "Oh, that's the wind blowing though the weeping willow leaves. It does sound kind of like a soft bunny whistle. But there aren't any bunnies here; you were all alone."

"No, I'm sure I've been with other bunnies. I could hear them nibbling the grass right next to me."

Timmer listened again, and this time he could hear crickets in the grass, eating and rubbing their legs together. They did sound a bit like bunnies munching. "Oh, those are only crickets in the grass. No bunnies here!"

"Oh," Karin said, her whiskers starting to droop. "But I could feel bunnies touching me as I hopped around. They seemed very friendly. So I really do feel that I wasn't all alone!"

Timmer looked around, wondering what could have felt like bunny-pets. He saw some willow branches hanging down near where Karin had been munching on the grasses. "I'm sure it was the willow leaves you felt. As you hopped around, you must have brushed against them. Come on and follow me; I'll take you back to where all the bunnies are." Karin followed Timmer until they joined all the other bunnies, and she was no longer alone.

That evening the coyotes were howling very close. The adult bunnies stayed awake all night long, running from one burrow to the other and checking all the entrances to make sure the coyotes couldn't get in. Karin and Timmer and the other young bunnies stayed down in the deepest tunnels. The next morning, after the coyotes finally went home to sleep, the bunnies came out of their tunnels to nibble the grass in the meadow. They were all exhausted from their sleepless night, so they were very quiet as they munched and chewed. Even though Timmer was also tired, he made sure that Karin was in the center of a large cluster of bunnies so she wouldn't feel alone.

In the afternoon, his mother sent him to run an errand. When he came back, the first thing he did was look for Karin to make sure she was okay. There she was, still in the middle of the big bunch of bunnies – but when he looked closer, he saw that there were big bunny tears running down her cheeks.

"What's wrong, Karin?" he called as he hopped over to her.

"Oh, Timmer, there you are. I'm sad because I'm here all by myself. No one wanted to eat or play with me today."

"But Cousin, you aren't by yourself." He wiggled his ears to point at the bunnies around them, then he stopped when he realized that she couldn't see what he was doing. "You're right in the middle of dozens of bunnies. Your mother is just a few hops in front of you. All your brothers and sisters and cousins are in a big circle around you."

"But I couldn't hear anyone. I thought everyone was mad at me and didn't want to talk to me, so I was trying to figure out what I'd done wrong. I felt so alone."

"No, you're fine. You weren't alone. Everyone was just tired out after worrying about the coyotes all night long, so they're being very quiet. Your whole family is here right next to you."

"I'm so glad you came and told me, Cousin. I thought it was all my fault that they were silent." Karin rubbed her whiskers along Timmer's face. "Thank you so much." Then they both bent their heads down and nibbled the young grass shoots together.

As Timmer chewed, he thought about Karin. *She can't see, so she doesn't know when she's alone or when she's surrounded by everyone else! How will she ever be able to figure out when to feel lonely and when to feel happy?* After that day, Timmer tried even harder to take care of his cousin. He would always be on the lookout so he could tell her where the other bunnies were grazing. He'd let her know whenever she would be alone, and he would come back from his errands as quickly as he could so that she would always have a bunny close by. This went on for weeks, but Karin didn't seem to be as happy as she should be. So Timmer worked even harder to make sure she knew when she was with other bunnies and when she was alone.

Then one afternoon, when he came back from playing with some friends, Karin wasn't by the bush where he'd left her. She wasn't with the other bunnies by the stream, or in the blackberry thicket, or in any of the bunny tunnels. Finally he remembered the meadow with the weeping willow trees, and he dashed over to look for her.

As he got closer to the meadow, he began to hear bunny laughter. Soon he saw Karin hopping around. She was dancing and twirling in the air and bouncing up and down.

"Cousin, what're you doing?" Timmer called, bounding toward her as fast as he could.

"Why, I'm dancing with my friends!" she sang out happily.

"But Karin, you're all alone here. There aren't any other bunnies in this meadow. They're all over by the stream, so you're here all by yourself. It must have been the wind and the crickets and the willow leaves that fooled you into thinking there were other bunnies here."

"Of course! It's the wind and the crickets and the willow tree I'm playing with," replied Karin, with her ears standing straight up and a smile on her face. "They're my friends too, and I've missed playing with them. They're my friends when I'm alone-but-not-lonely. Timmer, I know you've tried to help me by telling me when other bunnies are around or not. You've been working extra hard to make sure I was never lonely. But I've realized that sometimes, especially if I think I've done something wrong, I can feel sad and lonely right in the middle of all my brothers and sisters and cousins. I also discovered that I can feel connected to everyone and everything and be happy when I'm away from other bunnies, playing here with the crickets and wind and the weeping willow tree."

"You're sure you weren't lonely here?" asked Timmer.

Karin shook her head. "Not at all!"

Timmer did notice that she looked happier right now than she had in many weeks. He stopped and listened to the sounds of the wind and heard the crickets humming all around him. His heart felt warm and fuzzy as he heard them singing a welcome to him. He went over and rubbed his whiskers against Karin's cheeks so she could feel him close to her as he said softly, "I've been such a blind bunny! I've been so busy looking to see if you had bunny company that I never noticed everything else that is alive around us! Of course you can be happy here! Thanks for showing me what I was missing, Cousin."

Karin started tickling his ears. "Why don't you play with us, too? Come on, let's hop around and enjoy the meadow. If you bounce high enough, the soft willow branches will even give you a hug."

Timmer wasn't sure how a tree could embrace him, but he tried hopping up as high as he could. After several spectacular bounds into the tree, he landed back next to Karin and exclaimed, "You're right! The branches swishing around me as I jumped through them felt wonderful: it felt like the tree was happy I was inside it. Wow! I've never been hugged by a tree before!"

"Yeah, I love tree hugs too. And I never have to worry if the tree likes me or not. It'll always be my special friend."

"I hope you think of me as your special friend too," Timmer said, rubbing his ears along Karin's back. "Even if I was so silly thinking you'd be lonely without other bunnies around, and assuming that you'd always be happy surrounded by your bunny family."

"I don't mind that you've been a blind bunny," Karin giggled, remembering what Timmer had called himself. "Now let me show you around *my* world."

And the two bunny cousins, the trees, the crickets, the wind, and everything else in the meadow played and sang happily together all the rest of that day and for many days more.

The First Winter Solstice

✦

A long, long time ago, before there were humans or even many animals or birds, the earth was filled with all different kinds of plants. Every variety of green bush, tree, and grass loved the sun. Each day they would reach up their branches, leaves, and blades to the sun, honoring it and receiving energy and warmth in return. Every day was just the same as the one before; the sun would rise at the same time each day, and night would start exactly when it did the day before.

Then one year, the plants started noticing that the sun seemed to shine less each day, and the nights seemed just a little bit longer. The trees, bushes, and grasses began asking each other, "Have you noticed that the sun didn't seem as bright today?" "I thought the night lasted longer than usual." "I didn't get as much sun as I wanted today. Did you?" No one seemed to have any answers, just questions.

"We should ask Old Pine," suggested the oak trees. "Yes, yes," chorused the aspen. So they called to the wind to help them. The wind blew through the trees, rustling their leaves and carrying their questions from one tree to another, deeper and deeper into the woods. With a final, huge gust of wind, the leaves rattled their message into the very center of the forest.

There, in a small valley with a stream flowing in the middle and an open area where bushes and grasses could grow, stood Old Pine. Her top-most branches waved high above all the other trees. She was the oldest tree around; she'd been tall and stately when all the other trees were just sprouting up looking for open spaces to reach toward the sun. Old Pine heard the fears and worries that the wind carried to her, but she was quiet and didn't respond to their questions. This alarmed the others, because they had always turned to Old Pine for help and advice. Now not only was the sun in the sky for less time each day, but Old Pine wasn't talking to them.

Finally, after several days of quiet, Old Pine spoke. She didn't rustle her message through her branches and let the wind carry it; instead she spoke softly through her roots, asking the earth to carry her message to the other trees. "I have been noticing that the sun is in the sky less and less each day. I have been listening to what the other trees far up the mountain are saying. They too have noticed that the nights are longer. Everyone is talking about it throughout our whole forest, past the mountains and grasslands and into the neighboring forests. It's true: the world is changing, and our days with the sun are getting shorter."

This caused a great stir in the little valley. All the trees rustled at one another, and the grasses swayed and the bushes rattled their leaves. They could have communicated through their roots like Old Pine, but it's slower and harder to converse that way, and they were in a hurry to talk about the sun. It sounded like a great storm was passing through the forest as they all moved branches, leaves, and blades to cry their distress.

Old Pine heard their voices roaring through the forest, and she sent out her message calmly: "There is no need for alarm. The sun is not gone. We are still warmed by it. We can still grow our leaves and take in our energy as we've always done."

At that moment a cloud passed in front of the sun, and everyone shivered in the cold wind like they'd never shivered before. "No need for alarm?" squeaked the holly bush. "I'm scared!"

"What will we do without the sun? How will we survive?" the oak across the stream demanded.

"We need the sun to bring us light and help us grow," yelled all the grasses at once.

Old Pine tried to reassure them, but no one was listening with their roots so they couldn't hear her. The days went by, each one with a little less sun than the one before. The trees along the creek and the bushes and grasses in the meadow could talk of nothing else. Finally many of the trees, especially those with the largest leaves, declared, "We have talked long enough. Old Pine said we should not be alarmed, but what if the sun goes down and never comes up again? We must do something while we still can."

"If we have no sun," a maple tree worried, "we won't be able to nourish our leaves. They will all fall to the ground."

A chestnut tree wondered, "Perhaps the sun doesn't know this. Perhaps the sun doesn't understand how much we love and need its warm rays."

"Yes," agreed all the elms. "Maybe it's because we make our leaves dark green that the sun thinks we love the shadows more. We must send a signal to the sun so that it knows how much we need it to stay up in the sky." All the trees and bushes agreed.

"Let's make our leaves the color of the sun," suggested the maple trees. "We can make them all the shades of yellow, orange, and red."

"Bright yellow and flashy!" shouted the aspens. "So bright that the sun *has* to see them. Then it will know we love the sun best of all and it won't leave us."

Their idea spread, and the trees in the meadows and on the hills and even farther down the river all decided to do the same thing. "What do you think, Old Pine?" asked a young spruce tree, shaking its branches in alarm.

Old Pine waved its leaves slowly in reply. "Be patient and wait. The sun has taken care of us for so long. Should we not be faithful to it and wait a little longer?" So the firs, cedars, spruces, and younger pines all waited and kept their leaves green.

The maples, elms, chestnuts, and aspens all colored their leaves with dazzling yellows and reds, making the forest look like a fire was running through it. But still, each day the sun shone in the sky for less time than the day before. Soon all those who had turned their leaves bright colors could no longer hold them up, and their leaves began to fall to the ground. Eventually many trees and bushes stood bare, with not a single leaf left. They shivered in the wind that blew colder each day. Without their leaves, the maples, oaks, and aspens couldn't talk back and forth any more using the wind. The ground was so cold that it was difficult to communicate through their roots, so they just stood in the forest, scared and quiet. If Old Pine hadn't told the pines, spruces, and firs that the other trees were only sleeping, they would have been afraid that the leafless trees had died.

All the trees who had listened to Old Pine and still had their leaves, wondered what to do. There wasn't enough sun left for all the leaves. "Make them smaller," suggested Old Pine. She showed them how to shrink their leaves and make them very small and very thin, so that the tiny leaves needed less of the sun's energy to be able to cling to their branches.

Even with the long, slender needles that replaced their leaves, it was still hard to hold onto hope. Each day was shorter than the one before, and each night was both longer and colder. Old Pine stood calm and tall, and her peaceful presence helped all the others to keep their faith strong as the shadows came sooner each day.

The meadow and the forest grew quiet. Even the raindrops – which had once splattered noisily on the leaves of the forest and meadow floor – now froze into stiff flakes that drifted noiselessly to the ground. There were only a few trees and bushes left awake now. It was harder to rustle loud enough to talk with their thin needles in the cold air, so a few of them started whispering through their roots.

"There must be a reason," Sweet Spruce murmured through the ground to the other trees. "The sun loves us, I've always felt that. Why would it start going away like this?"

The firs sent their agreement. "Yes, yes, yes. Let us find the reason."

The younger pines were uneasy. "We need to find out soon if the sun will start coming back. I'm cold with only these thin needle-leaves."

In the middle of the night that was the coldest and longest any of them had ever experienced, Sweet Spruce thought she heard something in the ground. "Is that you, Little Fir?" she asked.

"Me? No. I thought it was one of the pines down by the stream talking," Little Fir answered.

"We weren't talking," said the pines, "but we thought we heard someone talking in the next valley."

"Shhhhh," said Old Pine. "Listen." So all the trees reached down into the earth with their roots and listened as deeply as they could.

It was more of a feeling than a sound, something they had never noticed before. But now that they felt it, they couldn't ignore it. A message was definitely coming to them from a new direction, from deep down below them.

"Yessssss," Old Pine said with a sigh.

Little Fir giggled, "Hee, hee! It tickles!"

"I feel it, I feel it," called all the pines by the stream. They were so happy that they waved their needles to tell the firs on the other side about their discovery. Soon the news was traveling down the rivers and up the mountains. "The earth, the earth," they all sang. "The earth is alive and it's sending us a gift of love."

"This is the same energy that the sun was always giving us," said Old Pine. "I've been listening for many days now, and I've heard this message from the earth, which is the same as the sun's: 'Here is energy and love for you. Receive it and grow strong and healthy.' The sun and the earth are related, but we were always honoring the sun and ignoring the earth. Now we must love and honor both." And the very next day the sun stayed in the sky a little bit longer than it had the day before.

All the singing and shouting by the needle-leaf trees woke up the leafless trees and bushes. They heard Old Pine's message, and they felt the earth too. "Why didn't we notice this before? It's so obvious. Even my thinnest roots can hear it," Serious Sycamore wondered to all who would listen. But most of the trees and bushes who had just awakened were discussing more exciting things.

"We must celebrate the earth and the sun together," all the elms proclaimed.

"Let's do something special to honor them," agreed the fruit trees. They talked and made plans, and the sun continued to stay in the sky longer and longer each day. The grasses got together and decided to grow in a tight clump so that they could send up a single long, sturdy stem. At the very top of the stem they put a circle of tiny grass blades and colored them all sun-yellow. After a few days of gleaming with the most brilliant color possible, the sun-yellow blades dropped one by one in remembrance of the time when the sun slowly went away. The top of the stem then burst open again, now with a glorious white puffball that looked like a huge snowflake. This was to honor the shortest, coldest day when the needle-leaf trees first heard the earth calling to them. Then the wind blew hard and the puffball burst apart like fireworks in celebration of the joy they felt in being part of the earth. The grasses were very proud of themselves, because they had just created the first dandelion.

Some of the bushes decided to layer their leaves in a circle and make them soft and colorful. They even made them smell nice. They had imagined roses into being! The fruit trees decided that, before they'd bring out new leaves, they would honor the earth with little flowers all over their branches.

It took a long time for the grasses, bushes, and trees to create everything they wanted to bring into the world. There were so many colors, shapes, sizes, and fragrances to play with. By the time they were ready, the sun was now up in the sky for as long as the night was dark. Old Pine suggested they call this day the "Equinox," because they were celebrating equally the sunny day and the earth's blessed night – or "Nox," as she liked to call it. They decided this day would signal the beginning of a season called spring, because this was the time that all the flowers would spring open. It was the largest celebration that had ever happened on the earth and under the sun. The earth wore a bright colorful dress to the party in her honor. And the sun smiled down at all the rainbow colors the plants had brought forth.

Old Pine also admired all the lovely colors. "This really is a wonderful way to honor both the earth and sun. It's so beautiful!"

"I wish I could have flowers, too," cried Little Fir sadly, shaking his needles.

"I tried to make some colors," said Stately Spruce, "but I was too tired after turning my leaves into needles and holding onto them through the long cold time."

"It's all right," Old Pine comforted the others. "The earth knows that we're the ones who heard her first and told all the rest. She knows that we love not just the sun but the earth, too." The other trees felt sorry for the pines, spruces, firs, and all the other trees who couldn't make flowers now. They decided to give them the name "Evergreens" to honor how they had stood strong through the coldest nights and first heard the earth speak her love. They called the day of the longest darkness the "Winter Solstice," because the sun (or Sol) seemed to stand still at its lowest point of the year. The sun decided to have a Solstice every year, so that all beings on the earth would have time to slow down, listen to their roots, and look deeper for what is most important to them.

Each spring, when all the other trees and bushes and grasses had flowers, the story was told of what the evergreens had done, so that they could also feel a part of the celebration. As the years passed and there were more birds and animals on the earth, the plants shared the first winter solstice story with them, too.

Eventually humans appeared on the earth, and they too were told about the bravery of Old Pine and all the evergreens. After listening to the story, a human elder asked, "Why don't we decorate the evergreens with all the beautiful colors of the flowers? We can hang decorations of orange, yellow, purple, and many more colors on their branches so they too will have earth flowers once a year."

Another human said, "Let's put lots of bright red ornaments on them, because many flowers are red and that will look spectacular against the dark green of the evergreens. And lights! We'll put bright lights in their branches to help them celebrate the sun coming back into the world."

"Yes," agreed the human elder. "From now on, every year we will decorate evergreen trees on the Winter Solstice. We will do this to honor the patience, hope, and trust that those first trees showed. And we will tell this story to remind everyone how important it is to appreciate all the loving gifts that nature gives us: the rich dark earth below that supports us as well as the bright sun sending energy from above."

The evergreens were thrilled by how the humans decided to honor them. Every year they rustle their needles, singing their appreciation as their branches are decorated.

The Change Wizard

✦

In an ancient book with a brown leather cover, there was a story written in thick, flowing, hand-written letters. At the top of the page were these words:

"By proclamation of King Jasper and Queen Maria, this is the story of the terrible change we made to the world. If you are a powerful wizard, please listen to what happened, and then search for a spell that will return the world to how it once was."

Then the story began:

High in the mountains in a land far away, there was a peaceful, friendly kingdom. Most of the people lived in small villages or on farms. There was one large city with a castle where King Jasper and Queen Maria lived. Everyone greeted their neighbors each morning, and everyone knew all the traders who went from village to village. When people wanted something, they would trade for it. When King Jasper wanted eggs for breakfast, he would ask Amanda, the royal cook, who would go next door to Paulo, who raised chickens, and ask for three eggs. Then when Paulo needed a new chair, he would ask Amanda, who would go exploring the castle until she found a nice chair in a vacant room. She would dust it off and take it over to Paulo. Queen Maria traded riding lessons for math lessons: the palace accountant taught Prince Kevan and Princess Cilla to figure with numbers, and the Queen showed the accountant's children how to ride a horse.

When someone had extra they would share with others who needed more, and everyone always seemed to have enough. No one tried to have a great deal more than anyone else. If they did, they were seen as being stingy and greedy, and no one would be kind to them when they needed something. The kingdom became known throughout the world as a wonderful place to live where everyone was rich and happy.

King Jasper and Queen Maria worked very hard to be the best king and queen the land had ever known. Sometimes they worried that things were not organized enough. They'd heard from traveling merchants that the best way to run a country was to have everything neatly arranged and categorized. The merchants complained that the one thing in the kingdom that was never orderly or efficient was the value given to the many different things they traded. In the fall, when the trees were full of fruit, a whole barrel of apples was equal to one shirt or two loaves of bread. In winter, if a person still had apples, they could swap just a few of them for three shirts or four woven mittens. Sometimes people would trade five loaves of bread for a chicken, and other times someone might give two chickens for a single loaf of bread. It all depended on what they needed for dinner that night and how many extra chickens or loaves of bread they had.

The King and Queen became afraid that because this method of trading was so inexact and changeable, something must be wrong with it. So they came up with what they thought was a magnificent idea. They asked the silversmith to make many small, round discs of silver with their pictures on them. Then they sent out a proclamation throughout their land stating that from now on, everyone would use these discs to pay for mittens, chickens, bread, or whatever they wanted. Instead of trading, everyone was supposed to pay exactly twelve pieces of silver for a barrel of apples, and a shirt would always be worth ten pieces of silver.

But the people laughed when they heard the King and Queen's idea. King Jasper tried to insist that Amanda use them to buy his breakfast. But when Amanda told this to Paulo, he laughed, "Silver discs! What are they good for? Why should I give you eggs for a bit of silver I don't need? Just take the eggs. I'll ask you for something when I need it. But I don't need any silver discs right now. Maybe if the chair you gave me gets wobbly, I can use some to prop up one leg."

The Queen and King tried to explain that using the discs would make things much easier. They told the people that it would be more orderly if everyone used the silver to buy things; then the prices would always be the same. The people listened and thought about it. "You know," Paulo told Amanda. "It wouldn't be a bad idea to write down when I give you a chicken, or when I get bread from the baker when she doesn't need eggs. That way we could keep track of things better and not worry if we didn't have anything to trade that day." He tried to make some marks on the silver disc with his knife, but they just made the King look like he had cat whiskers on his face. So Paulo brought out a scrap of paper and wrote "Six eggs for the King" on it and showed it to Amanda.

"Looks good to me," she said. They both smiled, then Paula folded the paper carefully and put it in his pocket. Soon everyone was using paper to write down when they gave something away and didn't need anything in return. Then they'd keep the paper and use it to trade with someone another day. Carrying pieces of paper was much easier than hauling around five liters of milk or a bushel of apples if you weren't sure how much other people might need that day. Everyone thought it was a brilliant idea to use paper to help with trading. Except the King and Queen.

"That isn't what we told you to do," complained Queen Maria. "I saw someone trade a piece of paper that said "One dozen eggs" for two shirts. Then the next day, the second person used the same piece of paper to buy three loaves of bread. This is more confusing than ever!"

"But it works," the people said. "We like it! Thank you for the suggestion."

"You're supposed to be using the silver discs," complained King Jasper. "That way everyone will know exactly how many discs something is worth, and we can write it down and keep track of everything precisely."

The people of the land just shrugged and continued trading as they had before, using slips of paper when it made things easier to remember. But King Jasper and Queen Maria didn't give up. They saddled their horses and set off on a quest to find the great Wizard Agatha, who lived at the edge of the kingdom near a vast forest. They explained the problem to her and asked for her help.

"I don't understand," Agatha said, looking at them with a very puzzled look. "What's wrong with how people are living now? Doesn't everyone have enough?"

"Yes, everyone has what they need," replied Queen Maria. "But it's so disorganized! We want to be the perfect Queen and King for our people. The traveling merchants, who have seen many countries and are very wise, told us that to make our kingdom better we must make charts and set rules for the precise value of every item. But we can't do that if people ignore the silver discs and keep trading however they please."

The Wizard Agatha narrowed her eyes and stared at them for several minutes. Finally she asked, "Have you thought carefully about what you're asking for? If I make a spell for you, I can't just change it back if you change your mind."

"Oh, yes! Oh, yes we have," said Queen Maria.

"We'll give you a thousand pieces of silver if you make the people understand the value of our discs," King Jasper offered.

"If this is what you truly want, I will do what you ask," agreed the Wizard Agatha with a sigh. "But I want three new blankets, a sack of flour, five chickens, a wagon, and two horses. You can keep your discs," she said, shaking her head and wrinkling her nose at the sack of silver King Jasper held out to her.

They eagerly gave her what she wanted, and Agatha promised to have everything ready in exactly one week. She told the Queen and King to have all their subjects come to town on the appointed day. Wizard Agatha arrived early that morning and set up a roaring fire in the center of the city square.

"This spell is so powerful that after people are changed, they will no longer remember how life was before. We'll be the only ones who will know that the transformation happened because of my spell." The wizard turned and looked sternly at King Jasper and Queen Maria. "Are you both really, really certain you want to do this?"

"Oh, yes!" they said.

As the people gathered, Wizard Agatha began pouring strange purple and orange powders onto the fire and chanting long, bewildering words in a language no one had ever heard before. The powders created a smoke that blew out among the people. As the villagers inhaled it, a dazed expression came over their faces, as though they had forgotten why they were standing there in the square. They slowly wandered back to their houses to go to sleep, even though it was still early and the sun was high in the sky. After the last of the people had stumbled back home, Agatha turned to the King and Queen and said, "I did what you asked. When the people wake up, they will value the discs you made. I still don't know why you want the people to do this, but beginning tomorrow they will. So I hope you enjoy the results of my magic. I'm off to go exploring with my new wagon and horses." With a quick wave she jumped onto the wagon seat, grabbed the horses' reins, and rode across the square.

"Thank you, thank you!" Queen Maria and King Jasper called after her. "Now everything will be perfectly neat and precise, and everyone will agree on what things are worth. This will make our kingdom the best kingdom of all!"

In the morning the people came together in the market square as usual to do their trading and giving, but now they all wanted silver discs in exchange for their goods. The Queen and King were happy to hand out the discs, along with a paper that told the people how many pieces of silver each item was worth. The traders coming into town liked the idea of using the silver to establish the value of the things they traded, and they told the King and Queen what a wonderful kingdom they had.

Wizard Agatha's spell had been so powerful that even a tiny whiff of the magic smoke made people value the silver discs. As the wind carried the smoke farther and farther away, more and more villages began wanting silver for their produce and other goods. The people in the city became very rich, because this was where the discs were first created.

As time passed, King Jasper and Queen Maria noticed that not everyone in their land was rich and happy. Some people collected a lot of silver discs, and they would make the prices very high for important things like eggs and bread, so that soon others had trouble just getting enough food to eat. This had never happened before. People couldn't store apples or bread forever and get rich, but they could store silver discs, and now some people had great piles of them hidden under their beds and on top of their bookcases. No one ever thought of giving a silver disc away, because they had all been bewitched into believing they were so very valuable.

The Queen and King even heard their daughter Princess Cilla say in a sad voice to her friend, "My mom and dad gave Kevan more silver discs than me, so they must love him more than they love me."

"Oh, no," moaned Queen Maria. "That's not what I meant when I gave Kevan the discs. I love both my children. He just needed a new riding jacket, and he's larger so it cost more than the one Cilla bought."

"I miss the days when people were generous and would just trade and give things away," the King said. "It's more orderly now, but it's not as nice and friendly as it used to be."

"We should have listened to our people," Queen Maria sighed. "They had the right idea about using paper. It was silly of us to insist on the metal discs. They're too hard to write on."

The King smiled. "I did look funny when Paulo tried to put marks on the disc Amanda gave him. He improved on our idea, and instead of listening to him I got upset and wanted it my way."

"I think we should admit we made a mistake and go find the Wizard Agatha and make her change it back for us. Then everyone will have enough again and be kind to each other."

When the Queen and King arrived at the wizard's house, they found it empty. The neighbors explained that, for some reason, when Agatha came back from her travels she didn't like the people in the kingdom as much as before. She decided to move far away and find a friendlier home. So King Jasper and Queen Maria went back to their palace and got horses and enough supplies for a long journey, and they set off to find her.

They had to pass through several other countries before they finally found Agatha's house outside a large town, near a gurgling stream. They told the wizard their concerns, and about how the people in the kingdom had changed. She listened, nodding and drumming her fingers on her wooden staff. "You should have thought of what was *really* valuable before you asked me to make people value the silver discs," she said. "I can't help you, because I can't change my own spells. I can only create them. No wizard can undo their own spell."

"That seems like a silly rule," said King Jasper.

"I agree," the wizard replied. "Long ago, there was a very powerful magician who was the leader of all the wizards. He wanted to be the most perfect leader, and he believed the world would be better if no wizard could change their own spell. He thought it was too chaotic. We would do some magic, then change our minds and undo the spell. Sometimes if we weren't sure about a spell, we'd go back and forth, casting it and reversing it several times. So he created a spell that made it impossible for a wizard to undo their own magic. After he did it, though, he realized the problems it created. But by then, of course, he couldn't undo his own spell, and none of us were strong enough to counter his magic. That means you'll have to find someone more powerful to try to cancel my spell and put things back the way they used to be."

Queen Maria and King Jasper looked far and wide for a wizard who could change the spell. They asked everyone they met where to find a powerful wizard, and then they searched out these wizards and asked each one for help. But none of them knew how to reverse the spell. "Wizard Agatha is a great spell-maker," they were told each time. "Her spells are so complex, I don't know how to change them."

As they sadly journeyed back to their kingdom, the King and Queen noticed that the smoke had continued to drift; so now it wasn't just their kingdom but every country they travelled through valued only the silver discs. Because they had originally asked the silversmith to make lots of discs with their faces on them, they had more than any of the other kings and queens. As they journeyed, King Jasper and Queen Maria began to notice that they weren't treated with the same friendliness as in the past. Some people thought they were very special because they had so many discs, while others seemed to mistrust them and wonder how they got so much silver. When they tried to explain about the magic spell, no one believed them. Only King Jasper, Queen Maria, and the Wizard Agatha remembered the way the world used to be before the spell.

When they arrived home, they realized that the only hope they had was to write down their story and send it out to all the countries of the world. Someday a great wizard might be born who would read this story and find a spell to undo their terrible mistake. Then everyone could once again live happily in a world filled with generosity and sharing.

Yin and Yang in the Mountains and Plains

✦

Once upon a time there was a pair of twins, a girl and a boy, named Yin and Yang. They lived in a small village with their family and friends. On one side of the village were hills leading to steep snowcapped mountains. On the other side stretched a vast, flat plain where their family grew vegetables. Every day when Yin and Yang played outside or walked through the village, they could see the tall mountains and the endless plains.

They were both very curious and asked many questions of their teachers and parents. They enjoyed solving mathematical puzzles and building bird-houses. They were fascinated by plants and learning how to grow them. But mostly, Yin and Yang spent their days wondering if it was possible to find a place where they could not see the plains, or to discover a place where the mountains were not visible. No one from the village knew the answer to that question, so one day they decided that they would each go exploring. Yang would climb as high into the mountains as he could, to see if he could find a place where there were only mountains and no plains. Yin would travel across the plains to see if she could find a place where there were only plains and no mountains.

They packed food and a few simple belongings, said farewell to each other and their family, and set off on their journeys. Yang climbed high into the mountains, but always he could see the plains stretching below him. The higher he climbed, the more spacious the plains became. Finally, he climbed to the top of a ridge and descended into a valley with a small lake in the center. When he got to the bottom of the valley, he looked around. Steep cliffs rose in every direction, surrounding him completely. "I found it!" he shouted. "Here is a place where there are only mountains, and I can't see the plains!" Exhausted by his climb, but thrilled to have already found the answer to his quest, he stretched out on his back next to the lake to rest. Soon he fell asleep.

Meanwhile, Yin was crossing the vast, flat plains. On and on she walked, but always she could see the mountains behind her. They were growing smaller, but it was at such a slow rate that she despaired of ever getting far enough away that they would disappear completely. Still she walked and walked. After traveling all day she could still see the mountains. As the sun was getting close to the horizon, she met a merchant journeying toward her from the opposite direction.

"Please, sir," she asked "Will I ever find a place where I won't be able to see these mountains?"

He put down his pack and paused, considering her question. "Where I come from there are also mountains. By the time you lose sight of these mountains here, you will start to see the mountains on the other side of the plains. Why do you ask?"

"I'm on a journey to see if there is any place in the world where a person cannot see the mountains and there are only plains," replied Yin. "Thank you, sir, for telling me about the other mountains. Now I have my answer. There is no place where the lands are all flat and the mountains are not visible."

"But there is such a place," offered the merchant.

"Where?"

"Right here. All you need to do is close your eyes. You will see no mountains, and you will be on the plains."

Yin laughed with surprise. Of course, all she had to do was close her eyes!

"Thank you so much for your help, wise sir!" she exclaimed. They bowed to each other, and he continued his journey. Yin opened her pack and prepared to camp for the night. As she worked she glanced at the mountains, smiling happily. She was excited to have found her answer, and was eager to tell Yang what she had discovered.

As the sun slipped below the top of the ridge of the valley where Yang was sleeping, a cool breeze brushed his face, gently waking him up. Before opening his eyes, he sighed, feeling a heaviness in his heart. When he'd gone to sleep, he was proud and happy that he'd found a place in the mountains where he couldn't see the plains. But now he remembered how much he loved the flat stretch of earth filled with rows of plants. He enjoyed watching the rabbits hopping and he loved to run there himself, playing tag with the trees. As he thought about the plains near his home, he could see them in his mind: his family picking vegetables for their dinner, his younger brothers carrying water for the plants. He imagined them so clearly that he could even feel the dirt between his toes, as though he was standing there right now.

Yang began to smile. The plains never disappeared, he thought to himself. They're always there. It doesn't matter if I climb high into the mountains and can't see them. I can feel them in my mind and I know they still exist. He opened his eyes and blinked. Then he blinked again. He laughed as his eyes wandered over the great expanse of the sky. The purple-tinged clouds waved at him, inviting him to play as they danced above him. As Yang stared up at them, he realized he was looking at the amazing plains of the sky. The sky was an even greater expanse than the earthly plains where he had lived all his life. Here was a vastness that he could always see.

"No matter where I go or how high I climb, you'll always be there," he said to the dark blue sky and shimmering clouds. It was too late in the day to climb the cliffs surrounding the valley and return to his village, so Yang took the food and blanket out of his pack and began making camp. He kept glancing up at the darkening sky, eager for the morning to come so that he could tell his sister what he'd discovered.

After traveling most of the next day, Yin finally arrived back at their village. Yang had already arrived and was waiting for her next to a row of sugar beets, his bare feet snuggled into the dirt. When they walked into the village together, everyone came out to celebrate their return. There was feasting and music. At the end of the meal they asked the twins what they had learned.

Yin told of her trek across the plains and how she met the merchant. "I discovered that something as enormous as a mountain will disappear if we close our eyes and pretend it doesn't exist. To not see something, all we have to do is close our eyes."

"Is that a good thing or a bad thing?" asked the villagers.

Yin hadn't through about it in that way before. She wasn't sure what to say so she slowly looked around the village. She noticed her older sister standing on the edge of the circle anxiously chewing on her fingernails, then she saw a friend who always seemed to disappear whenever the garden needed weeding. "I think it depends," Yin said hesitantly. "If it's a mountain of worries it would be nice to close your eyes and make them disappear, but if it's something you should do and plants or people need your help it's not nice to ignore them. So I think it depends on what it is and why you don't want to see it."

The villagers all nodded and smiled, pleased with Yin's words.

Then Yang shared his story of climbing the mountains and finding the valley. "The wonderful nourishing plains are always with us. But we can believe we have lost them if we expect them to always be in the same form and in the same place. Even when you can't see something you love, that doesn't mean it no longer exists."

Yin and Yang went to bed happy that night, pleased with the answers they'd found. Over the years they had many more adventures, and they both grew up to be wise teachers for their people.

The First Medicine Circle

✦

Coyote lived in the forest in a little wooden house with a packed-dirt floor and piles of soft leaves to lie on. Every day he dashed through the forest, crossed a grassy meadow, and ran down a hill to hunt on the prairie. When he finished hunting he climbed the hill, jogged through the meadow, and raced back through the forest to rest in his cozy home. Each day he followed exactly the same route, and soon there was a well-worn path leading from his home in the forest across the south side of the meadow to the prairie.

One morning as he was loping along his path through the meadow, listening to the gurgling of his empty stomach, his front paws hit something big and solid. All four legs twisted underneath him and he fell down hard in the dirt. He scrambled up and saw a round stone sitting right in the center of his path, completely blocking his way. The stone was so big that it touched the grass on both sides of his smooth trail.

"Who put this rock here?" demanded Coyote. "This is my path!"

No one answered. After much howling and complaining, Coyote went off across the meadow to search for the animal who had put that rock right in the middle of his path.

The first creature he smelled was Mouse. But Mouse felt Coyote's paws striking the earth and she hid deep in her hole. Coyote sniffed and sniffed until he found the opening to her home. Then he placed his mouth near the entrance and called, "Mouse, Mouse, come out of your hole. I promise not to eat you."

"No, no," cried Mouse. "I won't come out."

Coyote swished his furry tail in annoyance. Then he sat down next to the tiny opening in the dirt. "Mouse, this is much more important than eating." His stomach growled as though it disagreed, but Coyote ignored it and kept talking. "Someone has placed a large round rock in the middle of my path. You're in this meadow all day long, so you must have seen who did it."

Mouse stuck her nose halfway out of her hole. "I . . . I . . . haven't seen anyone put a stone anywhere. . . ."

"No! Not just anywhere. It's on MY path. And it's not a just a little stone: it's a huge boulder. Come with me and I'll show you."

"I can't go right now; I'm digging a new tunnel. The walls will cave in if I don't finish it soon. Then I'd have to start all over again."

"I can use my long snout to keep your tunnel open. Now go and find out who placed the rock on my path."

Mouse reluctantly crawled out of her hole and ran to the east to find Coyote's rock. For a long time all she could see were the tall grasses she had known her whole life. Then suddenly Mouse's nose bumped against the largest stone she had ever seen. "Oh my, oh my," said Mouse, as she slowly walked around the base of the rock. "Coyote was right. There's a huge boulder in the meadow!" On the far side she noticed that the rock was rough and craggy. There was an uneven cut running from the bottom to the top of the stone that made a perfect mouse-size path. She began to climb, going higher and higher. Hesitantly she crawled up above the top of the tall grass where she had always lived.

As Mouse pulled herself over the last ridge, her tiny legs gave way and she sprawled on the top of the rock. She lay panting for a moment, then her small black eyes darted around and she sprang to her feet. She could see above the grass for the first time in her life! Mouse saw a world she'd never even imagined existed. There was a thick dark forest around half of the meadow. She'd always thought the grass was tall, but now she had to stand on her hind legs to lean back high enough to see the tops of the trees. She twisted around and saw that the sky was wide-open above the prairie, which stretched to a faraway horizon. Circling around the top of the stone, she could even see a mountain peering out from behind the forest. Then she flopped onto her back and stared straight up at the white puffy clouds dancing above her.

Meanwhile, Coyote was getting impatient. He kept sticking his long nose inside the tunnel to keep it from collapsing, but the dirt made him sneeze. Finally he saw Mouse approaching, but before he could say anything she ran to him exclaiming, "Oh, Coyote, thank you, thank you! What a gift. What a wonderful rock!"

"Wonderful gift? What are you talking about?"

"From the top of the rock I could see farther than I've ever seen before. I saw the prairie and the forest. I even saw a mountain! I never knew the world was so large and so beautiful!"

"But what about my path? Didn't you see my wonderful path, and how the rock is now blocking it?"

"No," answered Mouse, closing her eyes to see the fantastic vision once more. "I didn't notice any path. I saw great expanses of grass, and trees reaching to the sky, and. . . ."

But Coyote wasn't listening anymore. He ran off to look for someone else to help him. When he got to the edge of the meadow, he saw Bear standing by a tree. *Bear is big enough to have moved that rock all by herself,* he thought.

"Bear!" shouted Coyote. "Why'd you put that big rock in the middle of my path? Now I can't run down to the prairie like I used to."

Bear swiveled around to see who was yelling at her. "What rock? What are you so excited about, Coyote?"

"The huge rock in the middle of the meadow!"

"There aren't any large stones in the meadow." Bear turned back to watch her cubs, who were climbing the tree.

"There's one now, and it's on my path! Come and I'll show you myself." Coyote tugged on Bear's arm, trying to grab her paw so he could pull her in the direction of his path.

"I can't come now; my cubs are practicing tree-climbing and I have to keep an eye on them." Bear stood up tall and shook her arm out of Coyote's grasp.

"I'll watch your cubs," said Coyote, pushing Bear toward the meadow. "I'll make sure they stay safe in the tree."

Bear hesitated, then she thought. *My neck is getting a bit sore looking up at the cubs. Maybe if I take a little stroll it'll feel better.* So she headed north, letting her head roll from side to side as she looked for Coyote's rock. Soon she came upon a round, flat boulder. *This must be what Coyote was talking about,* Bear thought to herself. *It's a very large, smooth rock. Lying here in the sun, it looks very inviting.* So Bear stretched out on the warm rock. "Oh, this feels good!" There was even a perfect bump on the rock to rub her neck against. As she gently rolled from side to side, she noticed that all her pains were disappearing. The longer she lay on the rock, the better she felt. Soon she was so relaxed she fell asleep.

Coyote was getting anxious. Bear had not returned, and the cubs had climbed down from the tree and were now playing with his tail. Finally he saw Bear approaching from the north. "Where have you been?" he barked. "Did you see the rock covering my path?"

"Oh yes, Coyote. Thank you, thank you! That rock healed all my pains. I feel wonderful. That's a very special rock."

"Did you move it so that my path is clear again?"

"What path? I didn't see any path. And I certainly wouldn't want to disturb something that gave me such a wonderful gift."

"That rock is not a gift!" Coyote yipped angrily, as he dashed off to keep searching for the animal who had put the rock in his way. This time he ran to the prairie, and soon he found Buffalo.

"Buffalo, Buffalo!" yelled Coyote, running up to the herd of grazing bison. "Did you place that rock on my path?"

"What rock?" snorted the leader of the herd.

"The gigantic stone that's on my path! It's stopping me from following the track I made from my house to the prairie so that I can go out and hunt every day." Coyote's stomach rumbled, and he swished his tail in anger thinking of that dreadful stone on his path.

"But Coyote, you're in the prairie right now. Why don't you just go hunting like you usually do, and make a new trail around the stone when you get back to the meadow?

"No! It's MY path! No one has a right to disturb the way I go to the prairie. You'll see when I show you the stone. It's awful and ugly! And you're big enough to move it for me. Come on, I'll show it to you." Coyote started off in the direction of the meadow.

"I would help you, Coyote, but I can't leave the herd right now. There are wolves around, and with so many young calves I must stay here and protect them."

"I'll stay and protect the herd for you, Buffalo. I can smell if my brother wolves are nearby, and I'll move the herd if they come."

"Very well," said Buffalo, knowing Coyote would keep asking and asking until he finally agreed. "I'll go see what I can discover about your stone."

Buffalo headed west toward the meadow in search of Coyote's rock. As he strode through the grass, he came upon a small boulder. *This must be the rock Coyote was complaining about*, Buffalo thought. *I'll just smash it to pieces and then I can go back to the herd.* He reared up and pawed the air, preparing to strike the rock with his hoofs. As he crashed back down, his hoofs hit the rock and made a thunderous sound, but they only left a small scrape on one side. Buffalo tried again and again until he felt his hoofs tingling. But the rock remained whole. *I'll try the other side,* he thought. Walking around the rock, his left hoof hit a big branch lying on the ground and neatly cut it in two. Excited, Buffalo tried stepping on a larger limb, and it too broke easily. Buffalo danced and bucked, feeling enormous power surging through his body. He lowered his shaggy head and struck the rock with his horns. Sparks flew from the tips of both horns. Then he reared up and bellowed to the sky.

Coyote heard his call all the way back on the prairie. *What is Buffalo doing?* he wondered. He wanted to run off to find out, but he had to stay and watch for wolves. He kept looking and looking in the direction of the meadow, and finally he saw Buffalo galloping toward him from the west.

"Coyote, Coyote! Thank you. Thank you, so much!" Buffalo roared. "I have gained much strength from this rock. My hoofs are sharper and my horns are more fierce and powerful. Now I can protect the herd, for I am the strongest of all the buffalo." And without another word, he ran off to show the herd his newfound strength.

All day long Coyote wandered, trying to find out why this strange rock was blocking his path. He asked eight more animals. Deer came back and told him how the rock had taught her to jump higher and faster than she'd ever done before. Otter thought that Coyote's rock was the best slide he'd ever found, and he played on it for hours. Owl solved many problems while perched on the stone. All the animals thanked him for the marvelous gifts they received from the rock, but none of them could tell him why it was there.

By now Coyote was very tired and discouraged. The whole day had passed and he hadn't gone hunting on the prairie, so he was very hungry. He slowly trudged back to the place on his path where the rock sat. "Stupid rock," he said. "Everyone else thinks you're so wonderful. But I'm going to starve with you blocking my path."

Feeling utterly miserable, he sat down, raised his head to the sky, and began to sing a sad song. Coyote sang on and on, louder and louder. Soon all the animals he'd talked to that day came to see what was wrong.

"It's this rock!" Coyote wailed. "It's still on my path, and none of you could find out how it got here."

"Why, this isn't the rock I saw," said Mouse. "That rock had an easy way to climb up so that I could reach the top and receive the gift of seeing the wide world. I wouldn't be able to climb this rock. Its sides are too steep."

"This isn't the rock I laid on," said Bear. "That rock was so smooth and comfortable that I could stretch out and sleep on it."

"This rock isn't the same one that gave me my strength," said Buffalo. "There aren't any scratches on this one showing where I struck it with my hoofs and horns." The other eight animals agreed that this was not the rock that they'd each seen. They were so puzzled that they all began wandering off across the meadow. Mouse headed east, Bear north, Buffalo to the west, and all the others in between. Soon they all had found the rocks that had given each of them a special gift earlier that day. Just then, Eagle flew over the meadow. From the sky, she saw Bear lying on a flat, sunlit stone in the north of the meadow. Mouse was dancing on top of a rock to the east, and Buffalo stood tall by a boulder in the west. Coyote was still wailing next to a large stone in the south. Along the outside of the meadow, neatly placed between each of these four creatures, were the eight other animals, each sitting, leaning, or standing next to a large rock. All together, the twelve animals and their stones formed a large circle.

Eagle flew down, circling over Coyote and calling to him. "Coyote, Coyote, I have seen a wonderful sight flying over this meadow. All the animals are standing in a large circle. Father Sky told me that such a circle would appear on Mother Earth one day, and here it is!"

"What circle?" asked Coyote and all the other animals.

"Why, the great Medicine Circle that contains all the different healing gifts for all the creatures of the earth. Have not all of you been given a blessing from each of these stones?" asked Eagle.

"Yes, yes! Wonderful gifts," chorused all the animals except Coyote. "But what is a Medicine Circle?" they asked.

"The Medicine Circle shows us how to find and use the gifts that are here on the earth for all beings. Each stone represents a different way to grow and learn in our lives. So when you need to see beyond your small world, ask for help from Mouse in the east, who has learned to climb to new heights to gain a broader perspective. When you need healing, seek out Bear in the north. For strength and protection, Buffalo in the west can help. Deer can help with agility and flexibility, while Otter reminds us to enjoy life, and Owl gives us wise advice." Eagle continued naming the other animals, the gifts they had discovered, and where their rocks were located on the great circle. She finished by saying, "Today all of you have found special gifts that you can share with all the other animals."

"Not me," complained Coyote. "I found no gift. All I got was a rock blocking my path to the prairie."

"Ah, but little brother," explained Eagle gently. "Your gift was the first one, and it is the greatest of all. For without you, all the other creatures would not have discovered their special blessings, and we would not be standing right now in the healing Medicine Circle that Father Sun and Mother Earth gave to us. Your gift was to bring the circle into the world. Here you stand in the south, as the trickster. You have the ability to trick the other animals and get them to do things they usually wouldn't do. Whenever you notice anyone traveling in just one direction, or thinking there's only one way to do something, you can place an obstacle in their path to stop them, just as you were stopped this morning by your rock. By preventing them from blindly following their old ways, you help them see a whole new circle of possibilities to explore."

Coyote smiled his toothy grin. "Yes, I can do that, Sister Eagle. Every day, as I walk around my rock on my way through the meadow to the prairie, I will look to see if anyone needs my special help."

To this day, all the creatures of the world can enjoy the many different gifts of the Medicine Circle. And Coyote still takes pride in playing the trickster, tripping us up when we get stuck in a routine, or when we think we know the best or the *only* way of doing something. Then, just like Coyote, we can explore a new path and discover unexpected gifts.

Magical Quakes

✦

Along, long time ago, back when dinosaurs wandered the earth, there was a giant lizard who lived in a jagged cave in a hillside. He was striped grey and brown, with yellow spots over his eyes, just like all the other lizards. He had a crest that started on the top of his head and ran in a pointy ridge all the way to his tail. It was hard and scaly so that his whole body was protected from any creatures that might try to pounce on him from above. He had four short, wide legs and a long tail that he could swing back and forth fast enough to knock down a small tree. He believed that he was better than all his lizard cousins because his crest was sharper and taller than everyone else's. He thought it made him look like a dinosaur, even though he was only one-tenth the size of a triceratops.

Every day he would go crashing through the forest, scaring smaller animals and rodents. Then he'd snap them up in his massive jaws when they tried to run away. Afterwards, he'd find a sunny rock ledge to lie on. Every night he would crawl back into his cave to sleep in the warmth of the earth. He loved his life, and he thought the only thing that would make it better was if he could somehow grow bigger.

One night, while he was dreaming of becoming a huge, ferocious dinosaur, he was awakened by the earth shaking. He heard trees falling and boulders rolling. He ran and hid in the deepest black corner of his cave. But even hunched in the back of the cave, he still felt the ground moving under his feet. Every time he thought it was over, the earth would groan again and he would shiver all over, making his crest rub painfully against the ceiling. Finally the ground stopped quaking, but he stayed hidden, afraid his beloved earth would start shaking again.

He didn't sleep at all the rest of that night, and when the sun finally rose it did not shine into the cave as it usually did. The rocks at the front of the cave that had been straight and tall, forming the sides of the wide cave mouth had fallen down, and now lay in a jumbled heap. As the lizard nosed around with his wide snout, he realized there was no longer a hole big enough for him to crawl through to the outside. It was only large enough to see what was once his wonderful meadow and sunny ledge now piled with fallen trees and rocks. He tried as hard as he could, but he was unable to move any of the rocks that blocked the entrance, nor could he find any other exit from the cave. "Oh, no!" he cried to the rock walls. "You won't let me go out any more to catch rodents to eat. What a cruel joke you've played on me! You saved me from the falling trees and rolling boulders, but now you've trapped me. I'll die in here!"

He began exploring the cave and noticed something new: a small spring in the back where water trickled down from above and out a hole on the floor. The hole was too small for him to crawl through, but it was large enough for a few bugs to crawl in. "This is even worse," the lizard moaned aloud to his cave, which was beginning to feel more like a prison than a home. "Now it will take me even longer to die, for I have water and a skimpy offering of bugs in the cave. Life is cruel, for it is giving me enough to live for a short time, while knowing that I can never run through the meadows and capture the rodents I need to really live. I will slowly starve to death – or die of the cold because I can never lie in my beloved sunlight again."

Slowly, as the sun rose in the sky, the lizard noticed how the rocks grew warmer. While it wasn't the same as lying on his ledge and feeling the sun bake his scaly hide, the cave was very pleasant. The lizard remembered that when he had first found the opening in the rocks that led into the cave, he had noticed how warm it was inside. Since he had never spent the whole day in the cave before, he had forgotten how hot it could get. He ate the bugs near the spring in the back of the cave and lapped up the water with his long tongue.

When it got dark, he settled down to sleep. The bugs hadn't really filled him up, and it was hard to sleep because he was still hungry. He heard a rustling by the entrance and realized that a rat was creeping into the cave. He lay very quietly, waiting until the rat was right next to his mouth, then he quickly snapped it up. Later in the night, another very fuzzy rodent came in, and the lizard ate that one too. Now he finally felt full, and he slept soundly the rest of the night.

The next day he drank from the spring and ate bugs, and that night three rodents sneaked into the cave. Three was more than he usually managed to catch back when he was able to run about on his stubby legs hunting in the forest. Lying still and waiting turned out to work much better for catching his dinner than chasing his prey ever had. *I didn't remember rats and other critters coming into the cave,* the lizard puzzled to himself. *I must have been asleep and didn't hear them come in.*

As the days and then the seasons passed, the lizard didn't die as he'd feared. He did complain a lot because he missed running, lying in the sun, and seeing the other lizards. It was also very uncomfortable moving around in the cave. Back in the farthest corner where the spring seeped in, the ceiling was very low and he was always bumping it with the crest that stood tall on his head and ran down his back. In order to reach the water he had to twist his head sideways to fit in the small space where the water trickled through. His tongue was growing very long because of how far he had to stick it out to lap the water.

"This crest is really getting in my way," the lizard said to walls around him. "I don't need its protection anymore. There's nothing in here to attack me from above like outside where the dinosaurs live." After a couple of days of thinking about it, the lizard decided to let go of his crest, even though it looked very impressive and had always been taller than all the other lizards' crests. He used to be so proud of it, but now the thought of being able to move around the cave without his crest was very tempting. He started to wiggle around, scratching it hard on the rocks above him. Because it hadn't been used for so very long, it had grown brittle, and it was fairly easy for the lizard to scrape off his whole crest.

Now it was more comfortable crawling to the back of the cave and drinking water and eating bugs. With his crest gone the lizard started noticing that his ears, which stuck straight up and were quite tall, also got in his way. He realized that he hadn't been using his ears that much. He could feel the vibration of the rodents creeping on the ground through his belly, and he could smell them faster than he could hear them – so the next day he rubbed his ears off. Now his head was smooth on top, which made crawling around the cave much easier.

Over the seasons and years, the lizard got even better at smelling rodents and bugs and feeling the vibration of their footsteps through his belly. Then one night the earth quaked again. The lizard cowered in the back of his cave and waited for the daylight. As the sun rose, the light coming in was dim and shadowy. "Oh no," the lizard cried to the walls. "There's even less room in here now. How will I continue to live? What will happen to me?" He tried to squeeze into the front of the cave to wait for rats and other small creatures, but he was too big to get close to the opening. "If I was smaller I wouldn't need as much food to eat, and I could move closer to the front of the cave," he said, and so he rubbed and rubbed against the sides of his cave until he was half the size he used to be.

His mouth was still very wide, and he had a big snout and rows of sharp teeth. He gave a long sigh and thought, *I haven't really been doing that much chewing. Mostly I just need to grab, swallow, and then digest the rodents. I don't need all these teeth.* So he spat them out all over the ground, except for a couple of long ones right in front that he smoothed against the rocks until they were very thin and sharp.

At night the lizard could sometimes grab a rodent if it came far enough into the cave, but he was getting more and more hungry. "Either this cave is too small or I'm still too big," he told the rocks around him. Then he shrank again, becoming much longer and thinner. But his head was still too large to get close to the creatures at the opening of the cave. Even after letting go of his teeth, his snout was still broad and boney. *Now if I could only think of some other way to smell my food,* he thought, *I could make my nose smaller.* But that was harder to figure out. When he flicked his tongue out as far as he could, he could almost reach the rats and other animals that came into the cave – and so he stretched his tongue until it was even longer and thinner. Then one day the lizard thought, *What if I put my nose on my tongue? I could smell through my tongue and make my head much smaller. All I need are a couple of slits to breathe through.* That night he ate very well because he was thin enough to slip right through many of the rocks piled near the cave's entrance, and with his new smooth head he grabbed three small rodents.

There was only one thing left about his body that reminded him of the big lizard he used to be: his four stubby legs. Most of the time he pushed them to the sides, because he wanted his belly on the ground to feel the footfalls of animals. The lizard really didn't want to give up his legs. They were the last thing that reminded him of his old dream of becoming a dinosaur. But they were getting flabby from lack of use, and they would get stuck on the rocks as he slithered around the cave. He decided to keep his long tail, because it helped him slither faster through the cave, and he used it to anchor himself when he reached for a rodent. But he really didn't have any use for his legs any more. *Ahh, I might as well let them go too. There's nothing here in this cave that I need them for.* He made a big exhale, and then slid along the cave floor, leaving behind a whole suit of skin with the legs attached. Now it was very easy to move about his home.

One night as he lay coiled in the back of the cave against the warm rocks, the earth shook again. This time the rolling and quaking went on and on. Even the rocks in the back were moving. The lizard whipped around trying to avoid the moving rocks. He slid very fast toward the small opening where the bugs came in by the spring. Quickly he was through the rocks and outside the cave for the first time in years. After the earth stopped quaking, he found some new rocks to hide in and waited for daylight.

When the sun rose, the lizard slithered out to lie in its warmth. It felt so good after the many years of living in the shadows. "Ah," the lizard sang to the sun, "how wonderful you feel on my smooth skin!"

"What are you?" a voice called from above.

The lizard looked up and saw a lizard just like he used to be. "Issss a lizzzard likesss yousss," he hissed. He still thought of himself as a lizard even after all of his changes.

"You certainly are *not* a lizard. Where's your crest? Your long snout full of teeth? Your legs for running and hunting? And you're way too small to be a proper lizard."

At first he was frightened and disturbed as he realized how much he had given up during the long years in the cave. But then a rat raced by. The large lizard tried to snatch it, but she was too slow. With a quick slither of his new slim body and his fast tongue, he easily grabbed it. *It's not so bad being who I am now*, he thought to himself. "Issss a newsss typessss of lizzzard," he told the other one.

"You sure can catch rats well. What are you called?"

"Iss callsss mysssself a ssssquake," he replied, thinking of how the earth's quaking had helped him create his new form. But without his old teeth, all the sounds he made came out more like a hiss.

"You're a 'snake'?" the other lizard asked.

"Yesssss, a sssssnake," he agreed, liking the sound of the word the lizard made.

To honor the changes he had made in his cave, all of the new snake's children and all of their children's children have always shed their skins every year. They do it to remember how important it is to let go of the things they no longer need. After they shed their old skins, they tell their children this story so that each generation will know that most changes are not as terrible as they may seem in the beginning, and that some changes actually lead to something even better than you could ever imagine.

Anna, the Mirror, and the Magician

✦

nna loved her house, her bedroom, her parents, her school, and especially her teachers. But she didn't like her older brother Bradford. Most people called him Brad, but when Anna was mad at him, she called him Bradford. Then he would start shouting "Anna-fanna-banana" over and over again, which wasn't fair because her name was just Anna and his name really was Bradford. Brad said she was "different," as if there was something wrong with not being the same as everybody else. He called her "stupid" and "strange," and said she played checkers and tic-tac-toe so weirdly that no one would ever want to play with her.

Anna did feel like she was different from other kids, though she would never admit that to Brad. Sometimes she liked to do what her friends were doing, and sometimes she liked to do things just the way she wanted. She was the only one in her school who liked mashed banana and cucumber sandwiches. Anna was the only girl who wore a purple rain hat, even when it was sunny outside. Being different sometimes felt great and sometimes it felt hard.

When summer was over, Anna was eager to start the third grade, so she wouldn't have to be around Brad all day. On the first day of class, the teacher,

Ms. Miles, led all the students around the room, showing them the reading corner, the sink for washing, and where to hang their jackets. She also pointed out where the extra paper and markers were stored in a cabinet in the back of the classroom next to an antique mirror. It was a full-length mirror with legs at the bottom so it could stand up by itself, without having to hang on the wall. Delicately carved arms reached up on either side to hold the mirror in the middle so it could gently tilt back and forth.

As each student paraded past they glanced at themselves in the mirror. When Anna got to the mirror, she stopped so suddenly that her best friend, Grace, who was right behind her, bumped into her. "Hey, keep moving," Grace said. But Anna didn't hear her. She was staring into the mirror. The mirror reflected an image of Anna standing there in her green shirt, dark jeans and purple hat. Her hair and face were just like they always looked in any mirror, but now, in the middle of her chest, she saw a gold, bronze, violet, and pink ball of swirling colors. She tried to reach out to touch it, but her hand was stopped by the mirror.

"Don't touch the mirror," the teacher told her. "You'll get fingerprints on it."

Anna tried to see if she could look down and see the colorful ball on her chest. But when she craned her neck way down all she saw was her green shirt. She looked back at the mirror and there it was, the swirling, multicolored ball right over her heart. The more she looked at it, the brighter and more colorful it became. By now all the other kids had passed by her, leaving her standing alone by the mirror. Then Ms. Miles announced that it was recess time, but Anna didn't care that everyone else went outside to run around and play tag. She stood still, gazing into the mirror. She noticed the colors changing. First they were bright yellow and peach, then they transformed into green like a field of grass, then blue like the sky. Anna wanted to reach out and grasp the beautiful ball of color, but remembering what the teacher said, she didn't try to touch the mirror again.

When it was time for the next lesson, Ms. Miles had to call Anna's name five times to get her attention and tell her to come back to her seat. Some of the kids laughed at her and made funny remarks about how long she had stood in front of the mirror. But Anna didn't care. Every chance she got she spent in front of the mirror. She stopped going out for recess with her friends. Even the games she loved to play weren't as interesting as looking in the mirror. The more she gazed at the ball in the center of her chest, the clearer and more magnificent it became. Sometimes it was like looking at the ocean, while other times it was like a summer sky with rainbow clouds flowing across it. Once it looked like a vast gathering of flower petals, and she was sure there a tiny face in the middle of it smiling at her.

One afternoon her brother came into her classroom. She had forgotten that her mother was picking them both up earlier than usual that day. Her friends had already gone next door to the after-school program, and Anna was getting one last look in the mirror before joining them.

"Here you are," Brad called loudly. "Do you know that everyone's talking about my dumb, stuck-up sister who looks at herself in the mirror all the time? Come on, we'll be late." Anna ignored him, as she usually tried to do. Brad walked over and looked at the mirror. "Hey, look at how weird this mirror is!" he exclaimed. "It isn't even attached right," he added, reaching over and swinging the mirror up so that it was pointing at the ceiling.

"Don't do that!" Anna yelled, trying to grab the mirror to straighten it.

"Try to make me," he taunted, swinging the mirror out of her reach.

"Stop it!" Anna screamed. "You'll hurt the mirror. STOP IT!!"

She reached for the mirror again, but Brad gave it a tremendous push and it flipped all the way around. Anna burst into tears, afraid the mirror would break as it spun around. The mirror slowly came back to rest in its usual position just as her mother walked into the room.

"What's wrong?" her mother asked.

"I don't know," Brad said, looking up at her with a serious expression. "I came in to check on Anna since she wasn't out front waiting like she was supposed to be. I found her standing here crying in front of this mirror. I was just trying to find out what had upset her when you came in."

"That was very nice of you to look after your sister that way. You're a very considerate brother," their mother said, patting Brad on the shoulder. "What's wrong, Anna?" she asked turning toward her daughter.

"He's lying! He hurt the mirror!" she yelled, pointing at Brad.

Brad stepped back and created a shocked expression on his face. "What do you mean? I was nowhere near the mirror."

Anna was so mad she went over and pushed him.

"Anna," her mother said sternly, "Stop that. Your brother was just trying to be nice." She took Anna's hand and pulled her out of the room. Brad followed them, sticking his tongue out at Anna, but only when their mother couldn't see him. When they got to the car, even though it was Anna's turn to sit in the front seat, their mother let Brad sit there to be "fair" since Anna had shoved him. Anna didn't think it was fair at all, as she hunched in the back seat. She wanted to go back and check the mirror, but she didn't know how to explain why it was so important to her.

The next morning when Anna got to school, she ran straight to the back of the classroom. The mirror reflected her brown slacks and yellow top and the purple rain hat she always wore. Right in the middle of her yellow shirt was a green, gold, and blue ball of color swirling faster than she'd ever seen it move before. Anna stared at the mirror, feeling her heart beat in rhythm with the ball's pulses. "There's stuck-up thinks-she's-so-beautiful Anna," Grace said, coming up behind her and speaking loudly to Carmen. "She doesn't play with her friends anymore. Just looks at herself in that stupid mirror."

"I'm not stuck-up," cried Anna. "I just like this mirror." She didn't want to say anything more about the mirror, because if anyone in the class was stuck-up, she thought it was Carmen.

"Come on, Carmen," Grace said. "Let's go sit over here together." Anna usually sat next to Grace. Tears rolled down her checks as she watched Grace walk arm-in-arm with Carmen. She turned back to the mirror and looked at the deep blue-black color in the middle of her chest. There were tiny lights twinkling at her as though she was looking at a night sky.

She sighed heavily, asking herself, *Why do I keep staring at this mirror when stupid Bradford teases me, Mom doesn't believe me, and now Grace doesn't like me anymore?* In answer to her silent question, red and gold colors started exploding in the ball like fireworks. Anna smiled at the brilliance of the strands of color flowing through the black background, surrounded by the yellow of her shirt. *I guess I like seeing that there's so much beauty inside me,* she thought to herself.

"Anna," Ms. Miles called. "Please take your seat. I have something very special to share with everyone." Anna reluctantly took a last look at the colors bouncing around inside her, then found a seat on the opposite side of the classroom from Grace and Carmen. The teacher announced that every class in the school was going to do a play about nature. Each class would perform their play for the entire school at the assembly next month. Anna's class was going to show how plants grew.

Ms. Miles gave everyone a part in the play. Weeks ago, the class had planted acorns in paper cups with dirt in them and had been watering them daily. Now there were little green shoots coming up with tiny leaves on them. Some of the kids were going to explain how water and sunlight helped the plant to grow. Anna was going to demonstrate how the plant got food from its seed. Ms. Miles explained that she would need to pull the plant out of the dirt to show how the seed was attached to the plant. Then she would wipe the dirt off and pass it around so everyone could touch it. "But what if they break the seed off?" Anna asked.

"That's okay. We have lots more plants growing," her teacher responded.

"But it will die if we do that. I don't want to do it." Anna protested.

"Do you want to do the part about the sun and have Carmen do the seed part?" Ms. Miles asked.

"No, I don't want anyone pulling the plant out and letting the seed break off."

"Well, that's how the play was written," her teacher explained. "We'll be performing it for the rest of the school, so it's important that we do all the parts, just as they're supposed to be done. Your brother was in this play three years ago and he did his part very well."

Anna hated being compared to Brad. Everyone always told her that he did everything just right. She'd been getting in trouble a lot lately for standing in front of the mirror when she was supposed to be writing or drawing, so she agreed to do the part in the play. She wanted Ms. Miles to like her, so she tried really hard to push away the yucky feeling inside when she imagined the seed falling off the plant. All week she told herself it would be okay to pull the plant out of the cup and pass it around and not care what happened to it. She was focusing so much on the plant, she didn't even go to the mirror for three days. The day before the play the teacher had them practice their parts. Ms. Miles moved the mirror to the front of the class so each student could see themselves as they practiced.

When it was Anna's turn, she brought her plant with her to the front of the class. First she looked at the teacher and remembered how much she wanted to do this right. Then she turned toward the class and saw her reflection in the mirror. She almost dropped the plant when she saw that the colorful ball inside her was now dull and grey. It was so faint that if she wasn't so used to seeing it she wouldn't have noticed it at all.

"Go on, Anna. Practice saying your lines," Ms. Miles said encouragingly. But Anna just stood there.

"You don't have to actually pull the plant out this time. Just pretend to," Ms. Miles said, thinking that Anna was still upset about what might happen to the plant when it got passed around the class.

But the teacher could not get Anna to say her lines. Finally she led Anna back to her seat and let the next student practice his lines. Later she talked to Anna about how it was okay to be scared to talk in front of the class and that lots of people felt the same way. Anna didn't think anyone felt the same way she did, because no one else had their secret, brilliantly colored inner-ball turn dull and dim. She was so afraid it might disappear entirely that she avoided looking in the mirror for the rest of the day.

When she went to bed that night, she dreamed she was a giant pulling up all the trees in the city. When she pulled up her favorite climbing tree, she woke up with tears on her face. It was such an awful dream that she didn't want to go back to sleep. She kept getting up and wandering around the house, being very quiet so that her parents wouldn't hear her and tell her to go back to bed. Finally, when it was almost dawn, she fell asleep curled up in the old rocking chair in the family room. This time she dreamed that she was talking to someone who listened to her fears and suggested new things to try. When she woke up she couldn't remember who she had talked with, but she knew what to do about the play that day. Before she left for school, she asked her mother for a clear plastic cup.

When everyone went to the auditorium for the play, Anna asked permission to go to the bathroom where she filled the cup half full of water. When it was time for the third grade to put on their play, Anna joined all her classmates on stage. When her turn came to step forward, she gently pulled the tiny oak seedling out of the paper cup, carefully brushed off the dirt and placed it in the cup of water. She passed it around and everyone looked at it and could see how the seed was still attached, giving the plant nourishment.

After the play Anna carefully lifted the plant out of the water. Holding the cup with the dirt, she poked her finger in the center and wiggled it around to make room for the seed and roots. Then she slipped the tiny oak tree back into its miniature pot. She added a bit of the water and packed the earth firmly around the seedling. The plant stood up straight and tall, just as it had before the play.

"That was a very creative idea, Anna," Ms. Miles remarked as they were waiting for the next class to start their play. "Now you'll be able to plant this oak with the others in the spring. Where did you get the idea of using the plastic cup?"

Anna started to explain that someone in her dream told her, but she still couldn't remember who it was, so she said, "I just tried to figure out some way that I could be in the play and the little plant wouldn't get hurt."

Ms. Miles smiled at her. "Well, you certainly did a good job protecting the plant."

Anna felt good hearing her teacher praise her, but it was hard for her to sit still and watch the other classes put on their plays. She wanted to run back to the classroom and look in the mirror to see what she looked like inside. Then her brother's sixth-grade class put on the last play about our galaxy. She was feeling so good about herself that she even admitted that Brad did a good job being Pluto as he ran circles around all the kids playing the eight planets.

Finally it was time to go back to class to get jackets and book bags and go home. As everyone else excitedly grabbed their stuff, chattering about the plays, Anna went straight to the back of the room and looked in the mirror. There she was, fully reflected in the glass. The mirror showed her purple rain hat, green shirt, and jeans. Right in the middle of her chest she could see a brilliantly swirling ball of blues, greens, and browns. She exhaled a huge sigh of relief, and then jumped backwards in surprise. There was someone else reflected in the mirror beside her!

She twirled around to look behind her, but no one was there. She looked back at the mirror, and standing next to her was a tall man dressed in black, with a green velvet cape that flowed from his shoulders all the way to the ground. He was wearing a purple cap and had deep brown skin and a very friendly smile. Anna couldn't help but smile, even though she still felt nervous having him show up in the mirror beside her. He seemed familiar to her, and the two of them looked like they were meant to be together standing side by side in their purple hats.

:You're the man in the dream who told me what to do about the plant!: Anna exclaimed loudly in her mind, as she finally remembered where she'd seen him before.

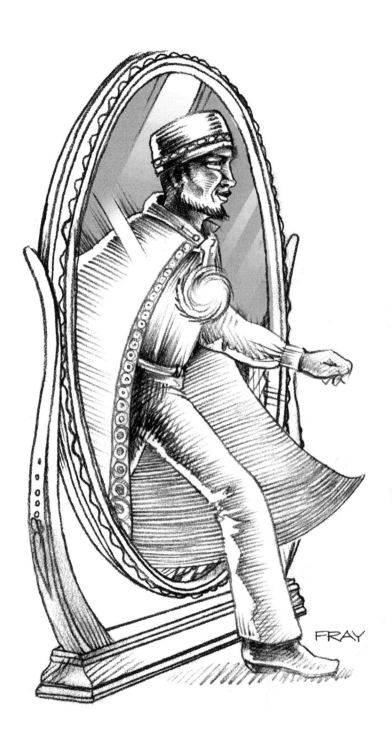

:Yes I am: said the man. Anna could hear his words inside her head. *:I'm called Marlinis:* he said, taking off his cap and bowing to Anna. *:I'm glad I was able to help you. And I'm glad you asked for my help:* Straightening up, he stepped carefully over the edge of the mirror and into the room. Anna looked around to see if anyone else could see the man. But everyone was busy getting their jackets and backpacks and talking with friends as they left the classroom.

:I have something else to show you: Marlinis said. He looked down at his chest and Anna noticed he had a colorful inner-ball just like she did. The ball swirled with bronzes and blues, greens, and golds. Even though it looked similar to hers, it felt different.

:I could tell ours apart if I had to: thought Anna.

:Yes, you're right. Everyone's Life-Glow is unique: agreed Marlinis. And to prove it, he reached his hand inside his chest and brought out the ball. It sat right on his palm, glowing. With some hesitation, Anna followed his example and drew out her own multicolored ball. Placed side by side, she could see how the colors flowed differently. Hers had lots of reds at the moment, and a deep shade of purple just like his cap.

:Oh!: Exclaimed Anna, looking back and forth between her ball and his clothing. *:It's called a Life-Glow?:*

:Yes, that's right: Marlinis agreed. *:We can connect and talk because you have a bit of me in your Life-Glow:* Then he pointed to a dot of dazzling red in his ball that was so bright it seemed to glisten, and the same color was swirling around in hers.

:And I have a bit of you in mine, too: Anna stared at his sphere, and it was like staring into the night sky. It reminded her of the play where her brother played Pluto. When she looked back at her globe in her palm, she noticed a brown that was just exactly the shade of her brother's eyes.

:Oh, yuck! I don't want a piece of him in me!:

:It's okay, watch: the man advised.

Just then she heard her brother call out. "Hey, Anna. What're you doing?" He came running into the room and stopped right beside her. "Oh, you're looking at the dumb old mirror again, Ms. Strange Stuck-up-on-herself." He looked around but didn't seem to notice Marlinis. "Hey, what's this?" Brad asked as he picked something up off the desk beside her.

With horror, Anna saw that it was the Life-Glow that had come from inside Marlinis. "Don't touch that!" she yelled at her brother. "Put that down right away!"

The minute she told him not to touch it, Brad immediately started throwing it into the air and catching it. Anna looked at Marlinis with alarm, but he was still smiling just as he had before. He motioned to her to look back at her brother. "This is neat. Where did you get this?" her brother asked her. Anna just stood speechless.

"Finders, keepers!" Brad stuffed the Life-Glow into his pocket.

"Give that back! It isn't yours!" Anna shouted.

Brad started backing away from her. "Make me!" He reached back into his pocket, then stopped, digging deeper and deeper, pushing his pant leg down toward his knee. "Hey, what happened to that cool ball?"

"You lost it!"

"No I didn't. It disappeared." Brad shook his head as though he was trying to wake himself up from a dream. "Wow, that was really weird. Well, I just came to tell you Mom called and she's going to be late. I'm going to be on the playground, while you stare at your ugly face in that stupid mirror." Then he ran back out of the room.

Anna stared after him, her fists clenched against her sides. Then the man from the mirror spoke into her mind. :*Relax. Don't worry about your brother. He took nothing from me, nor from you*:

:*Are you sure? Are you all right?*: Anna thought to Marlinis, as she tried to slow her breathing and calm her racing heart.

Instead of answering in words, he reached inside himself and pulled out another Life-Glow. He held it out to her and said *:No one can hurt what's inside of you. The most special part of you will always be special. That's the magic of it:*

Anna realized she'd forgotten her own Life-Glow in the terror of watching her brother toss around the one that belonged to Marlinis. Now she looked in the mirror and saw that it was right where it had always been. *:It got back inside me!:* she exclaimed.

:It never left: Marlinis told her. Anna noticed that he was holding his Life-Glow in his hand and that there was also one inside his chest. She cautiously reached inside herself and pulled out her silver, blue, and black ball. She glanced at the mirror. She could see her Life-Glow inside her chest, and at the same time it was also resting on her hand.

:Is it really magic?: she asked Marlinis. *:Are you a magician?:*

:Yes, I am a magician: he agreed. *:But this isn't really magic. If you look closely, you can see that everyone has a Life-Glow inside them:*

:Even my brother?: Anna asked.

:Yes, even your brother. Everyone's is different. Some shine more, some look like the ocean depths. Some are like the sky, or flowers in a spring meadow. Sometimes people's Life-Glows look grey and dim:

:Like mine was?: Anna said, remembering how her ball looked before the play. *:It looked all yucky and dull:*

:That happens when you're doing something that doesn't feel good to you. You were forcing yourself to hurt the seedling when you really knew it wasn't the right thing to do. Your Life-Glow loses its shine when you do something that you don't want to do:

:Like eating squash?: Anna asked.

:No, eating squash is okay because it helps your body. You still have to do healthy things that you don't like to do. Your Life-Glow will turn grey and dull when you do things that hurt you inside. Now that you know about your Life-Glow, you can check on it to see how a decision is affecting you. If you eat something

healthy that you don't like the taste of, or study when you'd rather be playing, your Life-Glow will still be shining with all your special colors. But if you lie to yourself or others, or you're mean and you know it, or you do anything that doesn't feel good to that special part inside you, you'll see the colors become dull and lifeless. All you have to do is look at your Life-Glow to see how something is affecting you:

:*And I don't even need the mirror anymore. I can reach inside and pull out my Life-Glow to check on it anytime I want to, right?*: Anna asked.

:*Yes*: Marlinis agreed. :*And you can also ask me for help anytime you need to. Just think the question in your mind, then listen carefully and I will answer you. Maybe I'll talk to you right then. Or I might come in your dreams. And remember, nothing anyone says can hurt this part of us that glows with all the colors of our inner beauty:*

"Hey, slowpoke, Mom's here," yelled a familiar voice from the classroom door.

"Thanks, Brad," Anna called back. "I'll be right there." She picked up her backpack and watched the magician step back into the mirror. He stood next to her, just like when she first saw him.

"'Thanks, Brad,'" her brother mimicked her as he walked over. "What's that supposed to mean, Ms. Anna-fanna-banana?"

"I was just thanking you for telling me Mom was waiting for us," Anna said smiling.

"So what were you looking at in the mirror? Your gorilla face?" Brad asked, grabbing the mirror and swinging it around.

Anna took a deep breath and, ignoring Brad, she reached inside herself and brought out her Life-Glow. When she thought of kicking and pushing Brad, the ball turned a muddy color. When she thought about how Marlinis had said that no one, not even Brad, could harm the beautiful ball inside of her, her hand glowed with the dancing colors from inside herself.

"Hey stupid, look at how far this mirror can swing!" Brad taunted her.

"Bradford, don't call your sister stupid. And be careful with that mirror!" their mother said sternly, walking into the room. "What's gotten into you?" she demanded staring down at Brad.

"That's okay, Mom," Anna said, reaching her hand out to grasp her mother's hand. "He probably didn't have a good day in school today. I don't care if he calls me stupid. I know I'm smart."

"I know you are too, dear," her mother said, as she let Anna lead her out of the classroom. "Come on, Bradford," their mother called over her shoulder. "We'll be late if you don't hurry."

Anna turned back to look at Brad. She didn't stick her tongue out at him, even though their mother wouldn't have known if she had. Instead she looked over at the mirror and watched as Marlinis waved and smiled at her.

:Keep watching your Life-Glow: she heard him say. *:Remember, I'll be here whenever you need me:* Then he slowly disappeared, but Anna knew where she could find him.

Section Four

✦

Stories About the Stories

Magical Worlds, Magical Stories

✦

I learned about the magical world around me and how I was connected to all beings from my teacher and adopted father, Red Eagle. He was a Mescalero Apache Medicine Man who taught me and others by telling stories and doing ceremonies. We would gather in his living room and listen as he described his adventures growing up on the reservation with his grandfather, who was a Medicine Man and Red Eagle's teacher. He showed us what *not* to do at ceremonies by telling us funny tales about a man who once attended a Medicine Wheel gathering and did everything wrong. I'd recently graduated from college with a BA in Psychology and Religion, and I was looking for lessons that I could write down and memorize. Instead, I received stories and an understanding of the world far deeper than anything I had ever learned from textbooks.

After apprenticing with Red Eagle for several years, I moved to Northern California to get my Masters Degree in Counseling. When people heard about my studies with a Native American Medicine Man, they would ask me to perform ceremonies for healing or guidance. When I helped them, I would share stories of my experiences with Red Eagle. I also related the stories he told me, especially the magical ones about healing. Hearing accounts about people whose tumors had disappeared and whose illnesses had vanished often helped open people's minds to the possibility that their own disease might go away.

In 1989, a friend suggested that I present a workshop at a local conference on shamanism and healing. He gave me a brochure and urged me to contact the leader, Dr. Ruth-Inge Heinze. I wrote a letter to her describing my background and interests, and was invited to present at the Seventh Annual International Conference on the Study of Shamanism and Alternative Modes of Healing.

The topic I chose was "Learning Shamanism through Storytelling and Experience." I'd never made a formal presentation before. My mind was exploding with questions: *Did I know enough to present at an international conference? What would I say? How would the people respond?* Since Red Eagle taught by using stories, and I had lots of experience telling stories to large groups of people, I decided to pick one to use as the basis for my talk. Also, it didn't seem appropriate for me to give a formal lecture on learning shamanism, since everything I knew about it was based on personal experience.

One of the things I didn't realize about the conference was that presenters were all expected to submit their papers in advance, preferably a few months before the conference. This was so that all the presentations could be published in a book that would be made available to the public.

When Red Eagle gave his talks, he never used a script or wrote anything down. I assumed I'd do the same. I'd tell a story, relate some experiences, and add anything else that came to me as I was speaking. But on July 1, exactly two months before the conference, I got a call from Dr. Heinze asking for my paper. I told her that I hadn't written it down yet. I tried to avoid admitting that I didn't even know what I was going to talk about. The worst thing was that I was having trouble finding an appropriate story. None of the books I was searching through had the right one. I started asking people and listening to their stories, but still, nothing seemed to fit. As the time grew closer, I got more calls asking for my paper. I did write a short introduction, but without knowing what the story would be I couldn't do much preparation for my talk. Dr. Heinze finally relented when I assured her that I would absolutely bring my paper to the conference.

After making that promise to the conference leader, I was very concerned when two weeks before I was to present I still hadn't found a story. I tried making one up, but it didn't feel right. I tried to patch together a jumble of assorted tales from my experiences with Red Eagle. But I felt totally inadequate offering it as a workshop about learning shamanism and storytelling. Finally, five days before the conference, I set aside the day for fasting and prayers and to focus on the story. I went into meditation to ask for help. After my many urgent pleas went unanswered, I began to see the humor in the situation. I thought of all the distressed phone calls I'd made to Red Eagle over the last few weeks asking for help. They'd all ended in his assurances to "just wait and it'd all work out." *You'd find this really funny,* I thought to Red Eagle in my meditation. *You'd tell me I still had five days left. And why did I need to know what I was going to say ahead of time, anyway?*

I got up from my meditation pose and wandered outside to relax. I watched the trees dancing and the birds doing aerial acrobatics. A butterfly was hovering around some flowers I'd planted. Then the story came to me, as if a soft wind had blown a puff of cloud straight into my mind. The cloud rained words into my consciousness until I knew the complete story of: "The Little Girl Who Wanted to Know What it's Like to be a Butterfly." I later renamed it "Butterfly Girl."

After rehearsing it a few times to make sure I could remember all of it, I asked in my mind, *:Who should I say told me this story?:*

:The Circle of Grandmother and Grandfather Story Tellers: came the reply.

:Who are you?: I asked.

:We are a group of storytellers who live on what you would call a spiritual plane. Some of us have walked the earth as humans or other creatures. Some of us have been spirits for so many years, we've forgotten if we've ever been anything else:

Then I had to ask, :*Why did you take so long to tell me the story? I was afraid I would never find one for my presentation. And I'm supposed to write everything down ahead of time that I'm going to say. This is a Professional Conference I need the story for!*:

:*We didn't know everyone who was going to be attending. We needed to wait until all the individual intersecting paths were clear to us. Then we would know exactly who would be at the conference and we could decide on the precise story to tell you:*

Finally, I was able to formally write out my presentation and bring it with me to the conference. It was the first time I'd ever written down anything related to my teachings from Red Eagle.

After sharing "The Little Girl Who Wanted to Know What it's Like to be a Butterfly" at the conference, many people came up to me with comments like, "I've waited all my life to hear that story," "It felt like you were telling that story just for me," and "That's just what I needed to hear." So it seemed that the Circle of Grandmother and Grandfather Story Tellers were right to wait and see who would be at the conference.

Since my first presentation at the conference was such a positive experience, I decided to submit a proposal for the next year. The theme was going to be "Power and Balance," and I already had a story for it. I'd been giving talks about the Medicine Way to my local Unitarian Universalist Congregation. One day a friend of mine came to hear the talk with her four-year-old daughter Chelsea. I'd promised the little girl a story if she came. I didn't have one planned for that day, so I tried to think of one while my partner and I explained about the use of crystals and stones. Nothing came to me, so during the meditation period I asked the Circle of Grandmother and Grandfather Story Tellers if they had a story for Chelsea. They told me they did. After the meditation I began to tell a story, which ended up being "The First Medicine Wheel." I later renamed it "The First Medicine Circle."

The next year I used that story as the basis of my presentation for the Eighth Annual International Conference on the Study of Shamanism and Alternative Modes of Healing. Through the story I explored the difference between Coyote's straight path through the meadow and the circle of all the other animals and their different gifts. I related the story to dealing with obstacles and finding balance in our lives. After the conference, Dr. Heinze asked my permission to print both stories in a book called: *The Bear Knife and other American Indian Tales*. I was thrilled! Since I'd never written down any stories before, I'd never even considered having anything published. Now someone was offering to do it for me!

Several years passed, and I assumed that nothing had happened with the idea of publishing the stories. But when I saw Dr. Heinze at a ceremony in the fall of 1994, she presented me with a copy of the book: *The Bear Knife and Other Native American Tales*. I eagerly flipped to the pages with the two stories, and there beneath the titles in bold print it read: "Jan Ögren, as told by the Circle of Grandmother and Grandfather Story Tellers." Not only did the two stories appear in the book, they were both illustrated (with the same images used in this book). I was amazed to see an artist's visual impression of the stories.

I gave a copy of the book to Chelsea, reminding her that the story "The First Medicine Wheel" was given to me just for her. It was now four years later and she was in the second grade. Her class was studying the Native American Way, so her mother instructed her to loan the book to her teacher so he could use it for the class project on the Medicine Wheel. But when Chelsea came home from school, she still had the book in her backpack.

"Why didn't you leave the book with your teacher?" her mother asked.

"Because he already had one. He was using it to set up a Medicine Wheel in class," replied Chelsea.

When I heard this I was shocked. I'd always shared the stories with an audience. While I would never know everyone personally who listened to my stories, at least for a moment we were all together in one place. Even if the audience was large, I could scan all the faces and have a sense of knowing everyone who was hearing the stories. Now these stories were being read by people I couldn't even imagine. Even Chelsea's teacher was using "The First Medicine Wheel" in his classroom. Were there other teachers doing the same? Who were they? Where did they live? I missed not being able to see the expressions on the children's faces when they heard the story. But now more people could hear these stories from the Circle of Grandmother and Grandfather Story Tellers.

After Dr. Heinze supported and encouraged me to write out the stories, in addition to sharing them verbally I continued putting them down on paper. This has allowed me to share the stories I am told with an ever-widening circle of people.

The Coming of the Hungry Ghost

✦

I grew up with an intense drive to be perfect enough so that I could win the acceptance of my family and the larger world. Anytime I failed to get the love I craved, I blamed myself, and vowed to try harder and to do better next time. By the time I was in my mid-twenties there was an empty pit where self-love should have been. Heaped around the pit was an overabundance of fears of being a horrible, undesirable person who would never be acceptable to the outside world. I spent all my time frantically trying to avoid the mountains of fear and trying to fill the voids of love and acceptance.

In 1988 my friend, Red Eagle, a Native American spiritual teacher who was like a second father to me, came for a visit. He and his wife Badger Woman were flying up from Southern California to participate in a special weekend ceremony in the hills near my home. I eagerly anticipated this annual gathering. After moving from southern to northern California in 1984, I felt that I never had enough time with Red Eagle. This year they planned to stay with me and my partner for two extra days so that we could have some private time together. Many people wanted to meet with Red Eagle, both at the gathering and afterwards, so we arranged to open our home for a few ceremonies and events while they were staying with us.

A man I'll call Paul had been at Red Eagle's side at every opportunity all weekend. He spent all day Monday at our house for a ceremony and class, which had extended late into the evening. Tuesday afternoon was another open teaching session. When the time came for people to leave, Paul begged Red Eagle to allow him to come back once more to see him. That evening was the only opportunity for just the four of us to be together: Red Eagle and his wife were leaving early the next day.

I fervently wanted Red Eagle to say no to Paul. I wanted time with my "father." But Red Eagle was very kind-hearted and said, "You can stop by after dinner, but you must leave early so we can have some time to get ready to leave the next day."

Red Eagle and Badger Woman went upstairs to rest while I began cooking dinner. They had just come down, we had given thanks for the food, and I was looking forward to some private time to talk when Paul showed up at the door. I told him we were still eating, but it didn't seem to affect him. He came in and perched on the edge of the couch near the table. He talked to Red Eagle throughout the meal while I silently ate my food. I was trying hard to be polite and considerate, attributes I knew Red Eagle valued and appreciated. As I cleared the table, I silently begged that Paul would leave soon so that I could have some time with Red Eagle. Then the doorbell rang. It was Paul's wife with their seven children, all of whom were under the age of twelve. "I promised to watch the children while my wife goes to work," Paul told Red Eagle. "I told her to just bring them over here."

Red Eagle looked at me and I shrugged. One of his teachings was hospitality. He opened his house to others, so I felt that I could do no less, so I waved them all into our home. "Thanks for taking care of them," his wife said, giving me a tired smile. "I didn't have time to feed them before we left. I hope that's okay," she added as she walked out the door.

Badger Woman went upstairs to pack while Paul led Red Eagle into our living room to talk. I looked down at the seven hungry, nervous faces surrounding me. "Wait right here," I told them. I headed upstairs with five of them following me. I grabbed all the toys and stuffed animals we had and hauled them downstairs. Then I arranged the kids in the dining room with the playthings while I defrosted everything I could find in the freezer. My partner was busy cleaning the dishes from dinner so I could use them again to feed all the kids. Luckily our small two-bedroom townhouse was on two floors, so the kids had a wonderful time running up and down the stairs. After dinner we played every game I could think of that wouldn't destroy the house. Paul moved outside to the deck with Red Eagle so that they could talk in private and not be disturbed by the kids.

I kept hoping Red Eagle would insist that Paul and his children go home. I was trying my best to be a good person and make Red Eagle proud of me, so I didn't want to complain. Thoughts of: *If he really cared about me, he'd send Paul home*, and *Maybe he likes Paul better than me* kept creeping into my mind, making me increasingly miserable.

The minutes turned into hours. My partner was dozing in a chair and Paul was still talking to Red Eagle outside. Most of the kids were lying on the sofa or sprawled on the floor. Then the three-year-old started screaming and thrashing about, trying to hit me, the other kids, and the cats. When no distractions worked, I picked her up in my arms and held her close until she gradually wore herself down into a quiet sleepy cry. Tears were also in my eyes as I realized what time it was: almost eleven o'clock. It was now too late for anything but allowing Red Eagle and Badger Woman to get some sleep before rising and driving to the airport the next morning. I settled the child on the sofa and went outside to inform Paul that it was far past his children's bedtime. They needed to go home and he needed to let Red Eagle go to bed. I must have been more forceful than usual, because it was only another twenty minutes before he came in, got the kids, and finally left. But not before asking if he could please come by in the morning before we left for the airport. I knew then that nothing would ever satisfy him, and I went to bed frustrated and very disturbed by his demands.

As I trudged up the stairs to bed, I felt devastated. I'd hoped to be able to fill some of the emptiness inside – where self-love should have been – with Red Eagle's attention and caring. Instead of hours together, we'd barely had a few minutes. As I lay in bed I wrapped myself in a blanket of hopelessness. I felt the bottomless pits within me demanding more reassurance and acceptance than I now had any chance of obtaining from Red Eagle.

The next morning I awoke with the "The Hungry Ghost" story in my mind. It was as though someone had read it to me over and over again while I slept, so that the story now felt familiar to me. I didn't remember ever hearing the phrase before, but I now knew deep in my gut what a Hungry Ghost was: it was the part of myself that kept me feeling empty. Every accomplishment, compliment, or special event would be gobbled up by the ghost so quickly that I wouldn't even notice it had happened. Then my inner-critic would fill my mind with a lecture about how it was all my fault that I wasn't getting what I needed and craved in life. That judgmental part of me would then suggest ways I could improve so that I could please others and obtain more goodies for the Hungry Ghost to devour once again.

Before getting out of bed, I imagined what it would be like to have a magical place inside that would hold feelings of being special and loved. The image of a green and gold vase came to me immediately. It had gently curving lines with tiny pictures of people dancing around the rim. It reminded me of a Greek urn I'd seen in a book when I was writing a report on Greece for my high school history class.

When I went downstairs to let Paul in that morning, I was able to smile at him and sincerely welcome him into my home. He stood in the entry way hopping back and forth from one foot to the other, anxiously peering up the stairway waiting for Red Eagle's appearance. He reminded me of Coyote, so eager to fill his sack with goodies that he had no time to appreciate any of them. I set out the coffee, cereal, and bowls and went upstairs to get Badger Woman and Red Eagle's luggage and put it in the car. When I came back inside, Red Eagle and Paul were sitting at the kitchen table deep in conversation.

I took my glass of orange juice into the living room and looked out the window at the field of mustard plants. There were wisps of fog dancing over the yellow flowers, and the sun was turning the air gold as it rose. I visualized my Greek vase in the meadow being warmed by the sun, and I felt my shoulders relax and my breathing start to slow. I began to smile as I thought of Paul. He was a perfect reflection of me and my struggle with Hungry Ghosts. By being such an obvious, exaggerated version of myself, he showed me how I would never allow myself to fill up with love as long as I kept surrounding myself with fears of inadequacy and scarcity. I breathed slowly and let the story play itself out in my mind again. Soon it was seven o'clock and time to leave. I imagined bringing my vase back inside and found a place for it in my chest, near my heart.

I drove to the San Francisco airport and let Red Eagle, Badger Woman, and Paul out near the check-in counter while I went to park the car. When I met them at the gate, Red Eagle gave me a firm hug and thanked me for all I had done for him. I felt the compliment settling into the bottom of the golden vase inside me; it felt like a precious gem shining its message of worth and beauty. As he was holding me in a warm embrace, I remembered the look he gave me the night before when Paul's wife brought over their seven children. Instead of the desperate, Coyote-like feelings I'd had then, I was now able to see the appreciation, understanding, and pride in his eyes as he'd looked at me and shrugged. Acknowledging all that, I felt another jewel materialize in my vase. The container had a long way to go to become full, but now for the first time there was something in it and no Hungry Ghost hovering nearby ready to gobble up the pleasant feelings. After Red Eagle boarded his plane, I heard Paul lament, "I can't believe he's gone so soon. I hardly got any time with him at all!" He gripped the rope closing off the gate so tightly his knuckles turned white. "What am I going to do?" he asked the empty walkway. "It'll be a whole year until the next ceremony!"

"Come on," I told him. "Let's go relax and grab some coffee. There's a story I want to share with you."

Shadow and the Dragon

✦

My partner and I searched for years for the right house to buy. We were living in a crowded development with a tiny backyard surrounded by tall fences. We wanted a place in the country that felt connected with nature, and we especially wanted an expansive view. Every place we looked at seemed to have something fundamentally wrong with it. There was a house with a fantastic view of the Sonoma hills, but it was built with the windows facing away from the view and toward the road. Another property was right next to a rose garden where the owners did aerial spraying with strong chemicals. Then our realtor suggested a place in town on a golf course. There was a view of the hills from this new house, but the yard was small and the neighbors were close-by. We decided to buy it, but after we moved in I questioned whether this was really the right place for us.

Our calico cat Shadow was in the back yard one day looking for birds and bugs as usual, when I noticed that she'd found a dragonfly. They were standing nose to nose on a long board that had been tossed into the yard, awaiting the day when I would have time to build a raised vegetable bed. The two were equally matched, both in size and by the intensity of their gaze. My cat was poised with her legs stiff and her tail stretched straight out behind her, with only the very tip twitching. The brilliant blue dragonfly was perched facing her: its wings were still and its long tail was also extended behind it, with just the tip curled. The board was six feet long, and together they took up the entire length. The insect was so large that I could easily see every bend in its tail and even the fork at the end. Shadow seemed curious but unconcerned by the creature, even though nose to tail it was slightly longer than her, and its wings made it much broader. I stood back watching as they stared at one another. The dragonfly rested gently on the board, appearing calm and unafraid of us. I was fascinated by how well I could see the lacy texture of its wings and how the head was like a giant baseball poised at the end of a long slender bat. Its spider-thin legs gripped the edges of the board, holding it firmly. The two continued to look intently at each other as though sharing a silent conversation.

It felt like a good omen to have this dragonfly show up to converse with my cat. The yard was dusty and covered with dead grass and broken concrete, so I hadn't expected anything from the natural world to be attracted to it. The former owner had used it as a dog run and had never planted anything in it. I planned to turn it into a garden once I had some time, but right now it offered little to interest an insect. *Maybe it would like some water*, I thought to myself. I wanted it to feel comfortable at our new home and come back regularly, so I went around the side of the house to find a flat bowl to fill with water. When I returned, the dragonfly was gone.

After the dragonfly's visit I felt better about where we'd decided to live. At least one of nature's creatures liked our back yard, even in its current abused state. I kept the bowl of water filled in hopes that it would return soon.

When people asked about our new house, I would tell them the story of Shadow and the blue dragonfly, describing precisely how the two were equally balanced on the board and how easy it was to see the details in the dragonfly's body. I enjoyed the story and told it often, always ending with how I hoped someday soon to step out the back door and see it perched on the new garden bed or on the benches we'd built around the deck. One day, in the middle of telling the tale for perhaps the twentieth time, one of the women in the group got an extremely puzzled expression on her face.

"But dragonflies don't come in three-foot-long sizes," she told me.

I stopped telling the story and thought back to the day I'd seen the huge insect. The realization settled into my conscious mind that never before or after that day had I seen a dragonfly as large as my cat. *That's true, they aren't supposed to be that big,* I thought for the first time. If people had doubted or been surprised by the size of the dragonfly in my story before I hadn't noticed. Now, instead of being focused on how the dragonfly had shown up to help me feel better about the house, I was more aware of its unusual size.

I continued to share the story whenever new friends came to visit our house. But now it'd changed and I began to emphasize the unusual quality and size of the dragonfly. This created a problem, because I wanted to visit with that dragonfly again.

When I'd first seen it, I thought it was very special but not strange or implausible. Shadow, the dragonfly, and I had all calmly and silently stood together in the yard for at least ten minutes, allowing me time to carefully observe all the details in the insect's head, wings, and tail. Now my perception had changed from seeing it as a special event to believing it was an extremely unusual and impossible experience. In order for it to occur again, the dragonfly would have to make it through my visual screening process that constantly filters the world, classifying everything as either "normal" or "not normal."

I've always been fascinated by how our brains work. I went to college because I wanted to discover the biological basis of consciousness. One of my favorite classes was Sensory Neurophysiology, where I learned that the senses are not focused on taking in data as much as they are attempting to screen out what is classified as irrelevant or mistaken information. There is so much more to the world that we can hear, see, and smell, but our senses are designed to screen this input in order to condense it into recognizable, understandable forms. As we grow and develop as children, our culture encourages us to develop our sensory filters so that they eliminate what others tell us is "not real" so that we no longer see it either. My filters didn't always work so well. Often I saw, heard, and felt things that others did not. But I learned to control what my senses brought in as much as possible, for fear of being labeled "crazy" and being sent to a mental hospital.

After graduating from college, in my early twenties I began my apprenticeship with Red Eagle. Because he was raised by his Grandfather on the Mescalero Apache reservation, his culture labeled things that Westerner's would call "magical" and "unbelievable" as "normal." Red Eagle teased me about how hard the spirit world had to work to get through my filters so that I could see more of the amazingly wonderful things in life. Too often my expectations of what the world "should" look, sound, smell, and feel like limited what I allowed myself to perceive.

Now that I'd labeled the three-foot-long dragonfly as "extremely unusual," I knew my chances of seeing it again were very low. I felt sad when I realized this, and I stopped telling the story. I didn't want to keep emphasizing the incredible nature of the event. I wanted to go back to remembering it as simply a natural encounter with a large, beautiful, blue dragonfly.

Then one day when I was in my backyard offering prayers of gratitude and welcome to the four directions, the dragonfly came back. Not only was I aware of its presence, I was able to hear it talking to me. I asked about its previous visit and how large it had been then. It responded by saying, :*You are not the first human to have difficulty seeing us in our full, glorious size. Let me tell you a story so that you'll understand that there are still dragons all around you – but we had to find a new way of being seen by humans:* Then it told me the story of *Dragon Magic.*

About the Author

Jan Ögren is an international author, storyteller, motivational speaker and licensed psychotherapist. She has apprenticed with Native American teachers for over thirty years, learning to walk in both the "normal" world and in the mystical realms. She lives in Northern California with her partner and an annoyingly intelligent cat.

www.JanOgren.net

Made in the USA
Lexington, KY
20 November 2019